DREAMGLASS DAYS
MARK HOWARD JONES

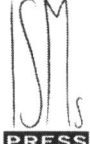

DREAMGLASS DAYS
MARK HOWARD JONES

ISMS Press
9 Dorris Street
Levenshulme
Manchester
M19 2TP

The right of Mark Howard Jones to be identified as Author of this Work has been asserted by him in accordance with the Copyright, Designs and Patents act 1988.

Photograph by Mark Howard Jones.

ISBN: 978-1-326-70981-5

To Rachel and Violet

Contents

Introduction 7

Fallen Star 9

Love Box 11

Dark In The Shot 14

Pig On The Beach 18

The Condition 25

From The East 30

The First Hours Of The Full Moon 39

Bitterbloom 44

A Million Miles Of Rain 47

Karas d'carcasse 51

Wunderkind 57

Sustenance 60

All The Fun Of The Unfair 65

Corpus Deliciosum 71

In An Ancient Embrace 76

Put On The Mask 80

Against The Grain 92

The Circus Of Automatic Dreams 101

Introduction

The stories included here were first published in the Manchester-based literary magazine Sein und Werden, which is the creation of its remarkable editrix Rachel Kendall.

They all appeared in the print or web versions of the magazine between 2006 and 2015, with the exception of one - 'The Circus Of Automatic Dreams' - which was commissioned especially for this book.

The magazine takes its title (which translates as Being and Becoming) from a comment about the relationship between Romanticism and Expressionism, made by the film critic Lotte Eisner in her seminal study of German Expressionist cinema, The Haunted Screen.

The magazine's stated aim is to "merge and modernise the ideas behind Expressionism, Surrealism and Existentialism". I can't say whether any of my stories meet those daunting criteria but I am very grateful that Rachel saw fit to publish them. I'd also like to thank her for giving this collection her blessing.

I've arranged the stories here in chronological order. Most of them were written to satisfy the theme of the then current issue of the magazine, but I can't now remember what those themes were or how successful I was in rising to the challenge set me.

One thing I do remember is that the themes were always intriguing, and allowed me to experiment with ideas that wouldn't easily have found a home elsewhere.

In my first story collection, *Songs From Spider Street*, I included several stories that had already appeared in Sein und Werden. I haven't reprinted all of those titles here, so this isn't quite a complete record. But I have put two stories in that can be found in the previous book - 'Love Box' and 'The

Condition' - because Rachel liked them more than any of the other stories I wrote for her magazine; so they belong here.

Writers are often asked 'where do you get your ideas from?'. I can't answer that because there is no answer, of course - we shop at the same ideas supermarket as everyone else - but I can safely say that all these stories are a hangover after having drunk too much reality.

Mark Howard Jones

Fallen Star

His finger ran stiffly down her spine, which flinched slightly under the pressure. The five broken vertebrae could clearly be felt beneath his fingertip. Half-pained she flinched under his hand, barely touching, writhing away as much as the pain would let her before settling back against his palm. The wires were tensile enough to allow her the illusion of escape but rigid enough to hold her in place. She sighed in a melody of regret and pleasure, knowing the day of her completion was a step closer. Her back would no longer hold her straight but it would hold her where she wanted to be.

*

I have to do this. You know that. I have begged you to find proper help. So now it must be this. He prepared the equipment and she smiled at him, making sure he saw the pain she mixed it with.

*

She was bound to have sustained some damage in such a long fall from grace but he would never have been able to anticipate the extent of the damage. Once he had opened her up, it became horribly clear what a long night he had ahead of him. Skill and patience would be at a premium.

*

The spine turned out to be a relatively simple matter after all, involving metal and pinning. After decades in the ice, her eyes were unpleasant to look at, if not completely useless. He'd known that, but their replacements were far from ideal - though adequate, he thought. An illusion was all that was needed. The stiff leather bracing could work wonders, within certain limitations. And the drugs, working alongside the auto-viral acupressure implants, would be a boon to her.

*

He was unhappy with the tension of her skin. And the dress, re-engineered at her insistence from her fourth wedding outfit, was not all his clumsy fingers could have made of it with a little more time. But he was pleased withe final result - given the constraints he had to work under. Her stricken star had had a long and damaging fall, failing and tumbling for year after year before the tragic end; yet he had only been allowed mere weeks to work his miracle. He nodded in encouragement as she propped herself against the cold wall. He was careful not to have any mirrors in the place: his clients would not appreciate that.

*

At last she was back where she belonged. The music began and the vibrant hum of anticipation died down as she stepped stiffly out on to the stage to a burst of horrified applause.

Love Box

Rie and I met at a social event organised by our company and we knew of each other's desire immediately.

In our haste to discover each other, we fled to the nearest place available to make love in this overcrowded city. Hastily and, we thought at the time, unwisely, we found ourselves in a nearby capsule hotel.

The 5,000 Yen cost of the room, and a sizeable bribe for the man behind the desk to forget he'd seen Rie, proved to be a very small price to pay for entry to paradise.

Both wonderfully supple and eager, Rie proved to be the perfect companion for lovemaking in such a small space.

Our room - barely three feet by three feet by six - seemed dauntingly cramped at first; particularly as, unlike most hotels of this type, there was a small door rather than just a curtain at the entrance of the room.

But Rie's flexibility proved to be a revelation. The positions that we attained that first night were both surprising and various. Our mutual joy arrived quickly but our desire was not easily sated; we got very little sleep that night.

We were married within a few months but found our sexual congress in the marital bed lacked flavour. We returned to our capsule hotel and rediscovered the heights to which our passion could climb. After that, we returned to the hotel regularly, often twice in a week.

Our limbs twisted into unorthodox positions that would daunt the fittest gymnast, but our desire for each other seemed to put the impossible well within our reach.

Ecstasy was easily attainable within our love box and, every time I released myself into Rie, it seemed to eradicate our lives outside that confined space. The restraints of married life, of my position as a salaryman, and of the capsule itself, dissolved into an ocean of love. Anything was possible for us.

It would have been a particular delight to have detailed our daring positions, recording them in our own capsule hotel Kama Sutra to share our joy with all, but discretion dictates that the manual should remain unwritten.

*

We have been keeping our appointment with love for over 15 years now. It is something that has perhaps gone on for too long.

Rie suffered terrible back pain following the loss of our baby six years ago. The problems following the dislocation of my hip during a road accident last year have not faded. Our bodies are no longer as young and as supple as they once were.

For over an hour now, Rie has not spoken. Condensation and sweat have made the narrow mattress sodden and my beloved has begun to grow cold beneath me. Try as I might, I cannot untangle my limbs from hers.

We last made love at 2.30 AM - just after the last of the drunken salarymen retired to his room. It is now 3.50 AM: I have grown soft and am no longer inside Rie.

I have only enough mobility to tap feebly on the door with my left elbow. My other limbs are locked tightly in Rie's love embrace. I cannot draw sufficient breath, doubled over as I am, to be able to call for assistance.

Checking out time is not until 9 am. It is possible that we will remain undiscovered until then. I cannot see how they will be able to extricate us even then; I imagine that several of our limbs will have to be broken.

I do not know which is worse; to be discovered like this, knowing the great dishonour it will bring upon us and our families, or to know that our wonderful love box will become our coffin.

Through the tiny window I can see the lights of a tower crane at a nearby building site. They waver as I struggle for breath, fighting back the urge to vomit, and my tears splash onto a patch of semen that has dried on the beautifully smooth skin of Rie's back.

Dark In The Shot

A personal response to some films by Paul Kirby

Journal entry, March 16th

After a brief credit sequence overlaid by some beguiling piano music, there follows a lengthy near-monochrome sequence of two men on a mountainside.

They are shown creeping around in the dark and appear to be searching for something. They are crouching and fear can be seen in their faces: evidently they are scared of being discovered and of having their task interrupted.

Often they lose their footing on the loose surface of the slope, which appears to be made of ash or something very like it.

The inadequate, crepuscular light is complemented by the indistinct, murmuring sound. Although the dialogue cannot be heard clearly, it seems to be neither the Australian English of Kirby s homeland or any dialect from his adopted France. It could be an eastern European language.

At the end of this sequence - the only extract shown at the special preview screening I attended - the one character seems genuinely terrified by the on-camera disappearance of his companion. If the man was acting, he was extremely convincing.

Like all Kirby s films it is enticing, hypnotic, stylish but disconcerting. It defies categorisation as the critics would say.

Can't see the wood , **Kali** *magazine, April*

Kirby s over-long Oakwood appears to confound expectations at every turn. His usual stylistic tics are missing, replaced instead by a luscious and extraordinary parade of set-pieces. Its tale of an expatriate mountaineer s attempt to conquer the highest peak of his adopted country is often taken as a metaphor for the director s own exile and ambition.

One critic has suggested that the film is a documentary about abductions and kidnappings and it is true that there are a large number of just such mysterious events during the film. The same critic cites the appearance in one shot of a copy of Rael Cesare s Dictionary of Disappearances, published in 1989, as proof of this. Yet no bibliography can be found that lists this volume.

Others have pointed out that if this theory were true it would be the only documentary that Kirby has made, to anyone s knowledge. Another argument points to the uniformity of the film stock and claims it indicates the footage was all shot by Kirby - and he would have had to possess phenomenal luck to have been on the spot when so many unusual occurences took place. Possibly Kirby s choice of non-professional actors for the lead roles has given rise to the documentary theory.

Like all Kirby s films, it is an enigma.

A different texture , **Evening View**, *April 19th*

Kirby s latest film is not a proper film at all but a compilation of clips from several of his other films.

Assemblage includes most of the famous sequences from the director s past work but with one important difference: either a vital line of dialogue has been removed or the sequence ends before it reaches its climax. In one section the lead actress face has been covered with a black mask - added in post-production - so that her facial expressions cannot be seen.

Several people in the audience denounced Kirby loudly and accused him of perpetrating some sort of hoax on them. They failed to understand that the films no longer matter to Kirby: he is simply using them to formulate his own algebra of absence.

Like all Kirby s films, Assemblage is a lexicon of loss.

Journal entry, May 24th

Fascinatingly, the notes accompanying the new DVD release of Kirby s fourth film, Renown , reveal that the diary shown throughout the film - supposedly belonging to the lead character - is Kirby s own.

Viewing the film again in this light, it is clear that many pages of the diary have been extensively revised or even ripped out altogether.

This tale of a down-at-heel composer who accidentally saves a billionaire from being shot during a bungled bank robbery and who then helps the man search for his missing daughter is my least favourite of all Kirby s films.

Kirby s final trophy, **Expressions** *pamphlet, June 6th*

The uxorious Kirby has only made one film since the loss of his wife to a hit-and-run driver in Copenhagen six years ago (the episode of the French ship-board drama Celeste that he co-directed is not usually considered part of his oeuvre).

He appears in Trophies often, lurking Hitchcock-like in

the background of a shot but never failing to stare directly at the camera; a tatterdemalion figure with a frowning, dark face. Nevertheless you have to know he s there to see him.

This tale of a proud horseman, deranged by the loss of his entire family to cancer, riding around the streets of Paris and causing havoc on the Metro until hunted down by the police is usually viewed as his personal response to tragedy. The extraordinary sexual content of the film can be read as a reaction to the loss of his own lifelong partner.

It is difficult to assess which Trophies either Kirby or his central character, Lescalles, think they have won.

Like all Kirby s films, it has not been made.

Since he recently vanished while travelling on the Tokyo underground system, this situation is likely to remain unchanged.

Kirby has become a page torn from his own diary.

Pig On The Beach

Even though he hadn't expected it to last long they had been together for nine years in all.

But now that Jane had gone - suddenly, cruelly, he thought - and their house was on the market, he needed somewhere to live. Somewhere "out of the way", he thought.

He'd always enjoyed his trips to the small seaside town as a boy and it was within easy travelling distance. A sea view was something he'd always wanted.

After work one day, he told his few friends over a drink.

"You don't want to move down there, man. It's dead," howled Alun.

Claire nodded. "Yeah. It's a bit old fogey-ish, isn't it? Full of geriatrics." He had to admit it wasn't much of a place. "Yes, but it's what I want...it's quiet."

Dave laughed. "It's bloody not, you know!" Dave enjoyed provoking or confusing people, pretending special knowledge everyone else lacked, so he ignored the remark and just smiled.

*

He was relieved the place was mercifully free of the usual British seaside tat. For once his childhood memories hadn't let him down.

As soon as he'd seen the vacant apartment on the seafront he'd liked its spare, stylish design and was pleased to see there was a vegetarian restaurant just five doors away. "This'll do me," he thought. "Just right."

*

He moved in during January after a miserable Christmas and a gloomy New Year. "New year, new start," he caught himself thinking, with a shudder.

It didn't take him long to get the place looking exactly as he liked it. There were only four small rooms to his "spacious executive apartment".

The big picture window gave him his dreamed-of view of the sea, beyond the esplanade and the broad beach. He spent the winter evenings staring out across the grey waves, listening to music and trying to forget who Jane was or had been. He always failed.

The morning she had left she'd spat the word "pig" in his face. One word - no elaboration, no explanation - and then she was gone.

He was confused. Why was he a pig? He'd always treated her well, listened to her, loved her. She sometimes grunted obscene names at him when they made love. It seemed to help her, though he found it distressing and uncomfortable. But that was the only time she'd carried her habit outside the bedroom, when it wasn't dark.

He couldn't decide whether she'd lost her mind or finally come to her senses.

*

The winter weekends were long and dark. He ate regularly at the nearby vegetarian restaurant, sometimes with friends but often not. They'd make the trip to see him with a mixture of pity and expectation in their faces.

He couldn't think what they expected of him, though Claire often muttered something about "moving on". He could tell they still saw Jane - why shouldn't they? - but they never mentioned her.

*

The quiet of the town was what he loved most about it. Surprisingly few cars drove along the esplanade road and his view of the sea was usually only interrupted by someone walking their dog on the beach or an elderly couple gazing at the waves from a familiar bench.

During his evenings of solitude the waves seemed to move to the rhythm of the Mahler or Sibelius he loved listening to.

Then the summer had come.

On his way to work one morning he noticed how the town had changed. It was more crowded, much noisier. The real difference had been hammered home to him on the first hot weekend of the summer. The beach, once beautifully empty, had turned into a puzzle of human flesh and pieces of bright material.

Fat families waddled by below his window, parents bellowing at children, while gaudy groups of thin, look-at-me girls giggled together on the esplanade. Jane had giggled in the same way when her friends had visited. He'd sat and ground his teeth as it brought back memories of teenage cruelty.

He began to hate the town as his peaceful haven turned into a monkey house of jabbering tourists. The majority of them lay around on the beach for most of the day, slabs of flesh in various states of disrepair and undress, desperate to turn red.

One Sunday towards the end of June the beach was so crowded that not a spare inch of sand could be seen between the packed bodies. Children played between them, impossibly, in spaces that did not seem to exist from where he stood gazing out of his window over the sands. He wouldn't have believed it possible to get so many people on one beach.

It was cruelly hot inside the apartment and opening the windows seemed to have no effect. What sea breezes there were refused to blow in his direction but he would not go outside, among them.

He returned to the large window time and again during the afternoon to see if the beach crowded with distant, identical flesh had begun to empty. But the holidaymakers seemed determined to cling to every last drop of sunshine. By the late afternoon he was convinced most of them had had their brains baked inside their skulls.

Intrigued by a column of smoke rising from near the water's edge, he rummaged for his monocular. It had once been a pair of binoculars but he'd dropped them while out birdwatching - a passion that had long since waned - and had never bothered to get the smashed eyepiece repaired.

Putting the good lens to his eye, he brought it into focus and scanned the beach for the source of the smoke. When he found it he could hardly believe his eye.

Had somebody really been trying to roast a whole pig in the middle of a beach crowded with holidaymakers? No, impossible!

Perhaps the animal had won its liberty from one of the small farms inland, he thought. Maybe it had met with an accident and someone had taken the opportunity to have a free beach barbecue. Idiots!

But that didn't explain why it was still whole, lying on its back with dead eyes destroyed by the heat. Or why its huge carcass was burning from the inside out. And why was there no-one attending to it?

He lowered the lens from his eye for a moment and wiped sweat away from his forehead. When he raised it to his eye again, the smoke seemed to have thickened and was no longer trickling straight up into the air. Now it was blowing across the beach. But nobody seemed to notice it in their devotion to sun-worship.

"Perhaps their brains have been baked!" he thought, as he caught a faint whiff of burning pork from outside. "Surely someone will do something soon."

As the beast's charred ribs began to stick out through the blackened skin, flames sputtered from its gut. The hot fat began to spit. A group of sunbathers nearest to the smouldering carcass suddenly jumped into life.

A young woman held a beach blanket in front of her exposed flesh to protect herself as her male friend waved his sunglasses reprovingly at the burning animal. Others had begun to notice the carcass as scalding fat hissed into their sunny reverie.

Then he recognised Dave and Alun rising from the sands. At their feet, Claire still reclined in the sun.

"That's strange," he thought. "They didn't say they were coming down today. I thought Dave had to go away." He felt oddly betrayed at the fact that they hadn't come to see him.

Then he saw why. Jane! Walking towards them across the beach.

And, barely a yard behind her, following, talking all the while, explaining, pleading, he saw himself. He, urgent, dark-haired, despairing. She, unaware and smiling ... but not at anything he said.

He gazed at the impossibility on the beach until the two figures were lost in the puzzle of people and the still-thickening smoke from the carcass. His heart found it hard to beat until he finally managed to draw in an urgent breath.

Sweat ran into his eye, stinging and forcing him to interrupt his urgent search for Jane and ... His train of thought was derailed by screams from the beach. Focussing the eyepiece he saw a small child, hair ablaze, running into the sea. Before he collapsed in the shallows, it seemed as though he was running towards a large ship on the horizon, arms outstretched to grasp the bright toy.

Safe behind behind his eyepiece, he searched the beach anxiously before finding his friends once more. Claire was making urgent movements, obviously in agony from the burns on her thigh and stomach.

Alun was desperately trying to smother the flames issuing from Dave's shirt with handfuls of sand as his friend struggled to take it off. The fire seemed to be getting the better of them.

He stood, panting in panic, trying to find Jane. Finally, towards the far end of the beach, in the surf, he saw her. She was running towards the sea, her hand and arm badly burnt, the ends of her long, brown hair smouldering. As she leapt into the water, it seemed as if she was about to take to the air.

He sobbed, frozen, staring like a one-eyed statue, as he saw the people he loved trapped out there beyond the glass. Even if he had a phone, he would have had no will to lift the receiver and dial for help as the beach, everyone and everything on it, blurred, brimmed over and streamed down his face.

Tears of relief mixed with those of terror and pain as he heard the high wail of sirens coming closer.

*

He had been standing there for hours as the beach had emptied or had been emptied by those who had arrived to help.

Frozen in the dimness, as night hurried towards him across the water, he could just make out the remains of the pig's carcass being lifted on the incoming tide.

The beast had burned out hours before but the stench of burning meat still filled the air.

*

That night, although he thought he didn't sleep, pink flesh blackened and blistered through his dreams.

The Condition

I wanted to draw the world, so I went to my window but I could only see a part of it. So I turned my pencil into a rocket and rode it all the way to the top of my disappointment. If you go to your window and look up, you can just see me, twinkling up there from time to time; geo-stationary.

The man sits in a chair. He cannot move and he is swathed in bandages. From what he can tell they cover him from head to toe. They cover even his eyes, with only a few cracks allowing him a partial view of his surroundings. The light is very low but he can tell he is seated in a room with bare walls and few features.

He doesn't know if he is ill, or has been in an accident, or if he is supposed to remember the details of either. He feels blank; his insides hollow, his mind unformed. He has no memory of colours or tastes or sensations other than those that surround him at this very moment; and he has no names to help him store them away in their proper boxes. If he cannot do this, he feels, then what is outside him might as well be as empty as what is inside him; even nothing must have a name.

Islands of memory seem to shimmer on the imaginary horizon in his head, far from where he is stranded. Unreachable and isolated. Is that where I should be, he asks himself? Is that where I can find out the answers?

The bandages itch and chafe and he wonders again why he is wearing them. Is he ill, infected? Wounded or burnt? He doesn't feel any pain, only irritation, but maybe that's because he is nearing recovery now. Perhaps his stay here is nearly at an end. Nobody has come near him since he awoke, but he thinks he may be in a hospital of some sort. Or perhaps a lazaret for those in a state of quarantine.

The palms of his hands itch but when he tries to lift his arms he finds that they are restrained at the wrists. His ankles are the same. So he might be a prisoner. Why else would anyone secure another person's arms like this? Maybe he would harm himself or others if they did not restrain him. So he might be in an asylum? Hospital, prison or asylum, he does not know which would be the worst of them.

If he could free himself he'd scratch like a monkey, though monkeys have more dignity. Monkeys, yes. He remembers monkeys but doesn't know if he's ever seen one. He wonders where they live and who created them. He imagines a green place where they might live, well-watered and with open skies.

A tree. He remembers something about a tree; he recalls what a tree is. There was something special about this tree, something on the tip of his brain. After several minutes failing to recollect what was unique about it, he gives up, groaning with frustration. His mind seems to be a ruin, with only vague ideas left standing on top of each other here and there.

Maybe he is dead, after all, and in a process of disintegration, decay. But he knows he wouldn't feel any discomfort if he was; he can't explain how he knows, but he does. Or maybe he is living a cancelled life, merely waiting to be recycled or re-assigned. That seems much more likely, he thinks.

Perhaps he has woken like this before, if there has been a before. Maybe he goes through this same tormented cycle over and over again. But he has no way of knowing, and that seems worse to him than having to repeat the same thing over and over and over.

There seems to be something moving in his bandages; tiny

things making only the very feeblest of movements but they are still unmistakeably there. He feels a slight revulsion at the thought that he is harbouring vermin. Perhaps he was wrong about being hospitalised; would a hospital allow vermin to thrive on the bodies of its patients? No, he has been abandoned, he now knows. He is nowhere. And no one.

Light. There is light at least. He can tell through the tiny chinks in the bandages over his eyes. The texture of the light has changed since he awoke. He has no way of knowing how long that has been; maybe days, maybe only hours. If days, then it must mean there are no nights here, wherever here is, the small window high in the far wall remaining constantly bright. No darkness, only light.

He knows his reasoning over this can't be right, something inside him reveals at least that, but it seems to make sense to him. There could be other reasons for the constant light but he cannot think what they might be.

He suddenly notices the smell for the first time. Now that he knows it is there it becomes overwhelming. His bandages are rank and filthy, he realises. They can't have been changed for a long time. And the things that are living in them ... are they feeding on him? He can't feel any bites or stings but maybe they are too small to be noticed.

Part of the discomfort, he now knows, is because he is sitting in his own filth. This accounts for the smell, too, he realises. No staff, nursing or otherwise, can have been near him for days, if not longer. He twists his head, trying to peer through the slits in the bandages. The room is virtually bare but for one other chair, giving him no clues as to where he is, or how long he has been here ... or when he might expect to be released. His heart sinks, his emotions in revolt at the knowledge that he has been so utterly abandoned. Perhaps, after all his conjecture, this is simply a form of torture for some act of evil he has committed and now blanked from his mind.

He could be in the hands of sadists, yes. They might be the tools of some dictator against whom he has spoken, despite the warnings of those about him. Or they might be just men, wise to commit him to this place and to force him to undergo this cyclical ordeal. The idea of power, its use and abuse, seems new but he knows it cannot be. If he is on some world somewhere he is aware that power of one sort or another is what chiefly occupies the minds and lives of its inhabitants ... if there are any.

Sound might give him some of the answers he needs. He opens his mouth and forces air through his waiting vocal chords. Immediately he is disappointed with the flat timbre of his voice, its light and unimpressive tone. Even his wordless groan lets him down, it seems.

Speech is a new toy to him. Words are a novelty, yet he seems to be able to call upon them, which makes him wonder how he knows their shapes, and where and why he might have used them before.

He gropes through the ruins of thought for the right shapes, the sounds that could be a lifeline to some meaning. He can't see anything much in this room but maybe there is another room adjacent to it, just next door. Maybe there is someone in that room and, if he shouts, they will hear him. And they might answer. He doesn't know if any of this is true but he invents something for himself - faith - to allow himself to believe it.

He exercises his jaw, groans loudly through his tight throat, and then draws in his breath ready to shout. His breath balances on the edge of action and then he lets it out, flying from him in a wave of vocalised anxiety: "Why am I here?"

Voices, a million voices; tiny, infinitesimal and individually inaudible, joining in one answer that vibrates through his body. The one answer that he felt he knew all along and that makes him weep with pity for himself, everything and everyone else, the tears soaking straight into the dirty bandages. "You are God," they say.

From where I was I had a perfect view of the world and wanted to draw it more than ever. So I changed my rocket back into a pencil, and tumbled down, down, ever down. If you go to your window and look up you can just see me, moving, twinkling as I spin towards the ground; high velocity.

From The East

In the city as ancient as the Romans, the old man hobbled slowly towards the remains of a shattered wall, his lungs still clogged by the dust remaining in the gritty air. Maybe it was his house he was breathing in.

Behind him the enormous steel arcs of the bridge lay like a huge lazy serpent that was once carried along by the Rhine's fast waters but that had now given up and beached itself in despair. Except it wasn't a bridge any longer. Not since the bombs at any rate.

Across the river the huge ragged Gothic towers looked down on him, sombre twins struggling to persuade the city's inhabitants that things were the same as ever; here lives God, be thankful.

The old man sat on the few bricks that remained standing one on top of the other and rested for a short while. Just as he was about to doze off for a few precious seconds, his peace was disturbed by a small voice. "Heinrich, Heinrich, Heinrich! We're here. Here I am and here comes Mama."

He took the little girl's hand and chuckled his hello, watching for her mother's approach. She wasn't visible yet but he knew what he would see when she rounded the nearby corner; her corn hair streaked grey, sallow skin which was once filled with peaches and pale blue eyes that had darkened so much over the past six years.

Slowly Traudl rounded the corner, treading carefully to avoid the rubble. She smiled weakly at Heinrich. "Hello, Heini. Are they here yet?"

The old man nodded. "Yes, yes. I've just seen them." Liselotte yelped with excitement, tugging at Heinrich's hand. "C'mon, c'mon. Let's go-ooo-ooo."

Traudl sighed to herself, tired out by the child's

constant energy. "Alright, Lisel, alright. We're going. Is it really free, Heini?"

The old man grinned at her. "Of course it is, Traudl. Who has the money to pay for things any more?"

The three figures set out for the place advertised on the poorly-printed handbills. 'Come and see the clowns! Bring back the laughter! Tuesday at noon, 23 Otto Gerig Str. Admission FREE.'

It had been passed from hand to hand among the townsfolk. This was something just for them, not a generous hand-out from their American 'liberators'. German clowns in a German city giving them something that Germans could laugh at. A taste of the old days and the scent of real freedom.

They scrambled over rubble where they had to but tried to stay on what was left of the road, dodging the jeeps and trucks shuttling the American troops to and fro from their barracks.

Traudl looked at the uniformed figures, wondering if her husband was still alive or not. She hadn't heard from Franz in three years, after he'd been sent to the Eastern Front as part of a Punishment Battalion, one of the so-called 'Clown Companies'. Coming just 10 kilometers to see little Lisel on her fifth birthday, without permission, was that so bad? According to the army it was.

She'd heard terrible things about the Eastern Front and had tried desperately to keep Franz alive in her mind. But she somehow knew she'd never see him again.

Old Heinrich grabbed her by the arm to help her around the edge of a huge bomb crater in a side street. The trio bobbed and stumbled to make their way past in the narrow space.

The last bombs had fallen just two months ago. Then the men in the khaki uniforms had come, saying they were friends. Liselotte didn't understand why friends would have destroyed their homes; old Heinrich just smiled at the smooth-faced young men with uncertainty in their eyes. After all, maybe they would do him a favour or two.

He remembers his old hands on the black and white keys and he's heard that these boys - for most of them are not yet men - like music. Perhaps they can find him a piano. Music instead of crying for a change; that would be nice.

Liselotte dragged along behind him, holding his hands. She wished Papa was here and she could ride on his shoulders instead, or laugh as he swung her around while walking along. But Heinrich couldn't do that, he was too old; Papa was so strong. But she hadn't seen him for a long time.

Climbing through the ruins of a house, nervous of the unstable walls to one side, they used the burnt-out shell of a car as a stepping stone down to the street. Traudl felt the shock of landing hard on the road shoot up her one leg and she stopped for a moment. A weariness, long held at bay for the sake of her daughter, swept through her for a few seconds and she barely stopped herself from crying. Things had been so hard for her on her own, as they had been for thousands and thousands of others, and the days were more numerous now when she ached for a man.

Even drunken, shouting Franz would do to warm the cold space in her bed, fill the empty gap between her legs. Sometimes she looked at the khaki-clad boys with longing but couldn't bring herself to do what some of the other women had already done; a fuck for a cigarette. What if Franz came back? What then? And what would little Lisel think of her mother whoring herself to an American soldier nearly half her age?

And if he ever did return, Franz would kill her. Him and his hot temper, his pride in his Gypsy ancestors, his honour.

She remembered after she'd looked at the waiter that time in the cafe. When they got home, he'd slapped her down onto the bed and straddled her, pressing his fist into her face. "You see this ring! This is a Romany ring. It belonged to my grandfather. My grandmother carried a scar on her left cheek where he used it on her for looking at another man. Remember that."

Then he'd pulled back his hand so she could take a good look at it. She'd seen it plenty of times before but he'd never told her anything about it. It was large and vicious and she'd always thought it too gaudy, with its large opal and elaborate silver work; not a man's ring at all.

He'd slapped her and ridden her viciously that night, as if he was breaking a horse.

After clambering over the debris of an old baker's shop, the three finally found themselves outside the address shown in the flyers. A simple printed sign on the wall showed an arrow, pointing downwards. "This must be it," said Heinrich, leading the way.

Down the cellar steps they found themselves in a large low-ceiling room, crowded with expectant people and smelling of broken pipes and burning oil from the lamps dotted high up on the walls. At one end of the cellar was a red curtain, hastily strung up to provide the illusion of a stage.

Lisel yelped excitedly and even Traudl managed to grin happily at Heinrich. They made their way to a couple of old chairs and a box and sat down as best they could, nodding to old neighbours and friends. There was a buzz of voices. The place didn't seem big enough for a performance.

After a short while a man appeared from behind the curtain, dressed in grubby top hat and a red ringmaster's coat with tattered tails. He was illuminated dramatically by the clusters of dripping candles set into alcoves at either side of the 'stage' area. There was a small gasp of excitement as he placed his hand on the curtain, ready to draw it aside.

"Good evening, good evening everybody. Thank you for coming. We hope you will not be disappointed ... by what we have to show you," he began before ducking his head behind the curtain to make sure everything was ready. His head emerged again, a lopsided smile on his thin face.

"My ladies, my gentlemen, my little ones. The clowns are back! Rejoice! Laughter and good luck have returned ..."

The man tugged a cord that brought the curtain falling to the floor. There was a sound of disappointed breath being released as nothing but a table was revealed.

"Ladies and gentlemen, do not be disappointed. Look closer. Look. Here are the clowns." The ringmaster ran his arm along a line of four large glass jars, filled with a cloudy thick liquid in which something floated.

Those nearest the front could best make out what was in the jars, and when they did a chorus of gasps and a single scream filled the room. This was quickly replaced by a buzz of excitement while those at the back hurled questions towards the front.

"All guaranteed, ladies and gentlemen. All from genuine clowns! A talisman to bring you luck and good fortune," continued the ringmaster. Excited children began to whine at their mothers for whatever was on offer.

Traudl was on her feet now, excited by whatever there was to be excited about. She held Lisel's hand tight and pushed forward, eager to see. Within a few seconds, she'd wished she hadn't.

She clapped her hand over her mouth as she saw four large, sealed jars sitting on a makeshift trestle table; they were filled with bits of people. The pieces of faces and fingers and chunks of flesh were still covered in greasepaint. These were the clowns. What was left of them was being sold as grisly talismen.

The fourth jar was the worst of all. In it a complete head sat. Dead eyes empty of laughter stared at her from the murk of the preservative fluid; red paint still covered the end of the nose but, where it touched the glass, it had begun to rot away, exposing the bone beneath.

The obscene things drifted placidly in the thick liquid, bobbing against the glass when the vibration of a passing truck disturbed them briefly. They were now mere emblems of ruined humanity, pieces of people reduced to artefacts to be bought and sold. Traudl felt suddenly as if she would vomit but fought against it.

She began to pull a protesting Lisel away; the child wanted to be part of the excitement, to have what the other children were getting as mothers began to haggle with the ringmaster. Hearing the discussion turn to money, Traudl changed her mind and shoved two protesting women aside sharply.

She pushed forward and pressed her face close to the ringmaster's. "My God, where did you find these awful things?" she cried. The man looked uncomfortable and Heinrich grabbed Traudl firmly by the arm. "Best not to ask," he hissed. "From the east."

The east? What was the old fool on about? She didn't want to hear about the east.

The east? She'd heard stories from the few lucky soldiers to return on leave from the Eastern Front. About secret places, secret weapons. But what could this grisly spectacle have to do with any of that?

The east? Where they'd sent Franz. Where the sacrifice of all their dreams had begun. None of this seemed right to her; Traudl grabbed Lisle roughly by the arm and dragged her towards the exit. "Come on, come on," she kept repeating to her chorus of childish yelps. The girl wriggled free and ran to Heinrich, who caught her in his arms. He winked to Traudl as she stopped and looked round, letting her know he'd fix things.

He hugged the girl tight and slipped something wrapped in wax paper - rarest of commodities - into the her hand. "Here, here. Don't tell your Mama, OK?!" Lisel looked up at him and grinned before slipping the object into her coat pocket.

"Go on, off you go. Your Mama's waiting." Heinrich watched as the two figures disappeared up into the dusty daylight.

*

Lisel's mother tucked her in and kissed her goodnight, drawing across the curtain that was now the only door she had. She heard her mother go across and put the radio on, softly, waiting for the news programme as she always did.

Lisel waited a few minutes until she knew her mother would be straining to hear the set's low tones, then she put her favourite doll aside and crept out of bed. Her coat was draped across a chair and she had no trouble finding it, even in the dark. The treasure was still in her pocket.

She took the precious parcel over to the window, where a little light still came in and pulled back the curtain a crack. Holding up the small parcel she carefully and slowly unwrapped the crackling wax paper, hoping not to give herself away.

When she unfolded the final piece of paper Lisel let out a little gasp and nearly dropped the object. She placed it carefully on the window sill and looked at it. It was an ear. A man's ear; it had hair coming out of it, like old Heinrich's did. After staring at it for a few moments, she turned it carefully with one finger. It gave off a strange smell, like she remembered from the hospital.

On the scraps of wet, ruined skin there were still signs of white greasepaint. Lisel strained to hear the music and the laughter her mother promised, struggled to remember if she'd ever seen a clown before. She didn't think so but she still knew that this wasn't what they were supposed to be like.

She felt disappointed. Why had Heinrich given her this? She'd heard it said it would be a good luck charm but she

From the East

wasn't sure if she liked it. Puzzled, she wrapped it back up and put it back into its hiding place.

It was a long time before she was able to fall asleep but, just before she did, Lisel thought of the other children and what they had been given. Tomorrow at school she would ask them. Maybe between them they'd have a whole clown.

*

The moon was up by the time Liselotte left her friends' house, the pale light making the rubble look ghostly and insubstantial. She knew Mama would be cross that she was so late but she was so excited as she scrambled carefully over some of the larger blocks of stone. She tried to put the scolding she would get out of her mind.

Liselotte couldn't wait to show her mother the treasure that she'd swapped with Hans and his sister. He now had her clown's ear and she had ... this. She thought she'd never see it again but here it was in her hand. She was filled with pride. Mama would be so pleased.

She tramped up the stairs and pushed the door open. Her mother was sitting at the table with a shawl wrapped around her against the cold. The old gramophone had its lid open, so she had been listening to music and her eyes were red with crying.

As soon as her mother saw her she wailed "Liiiisel!" But the girl strutted forward boldly and yelled back: "Mama! Mama! Don't be angry. I've got a present for you. Something you'll like."

Her mother's face took on an expression of surprise, her mouth making a silent 'Oh'. The girl's eyes glittered as she reached into her coat pocket for the treasure that she was sure would delight her mother. She unwrapped it and placed it carefully on the table in front of her mother.

Traudl stood up, pushing the chair back roughly. She felt sick, she felt angry, scared. Her daughter had just placed a severed human finger in front of her as if it had been a precious bar of chocolate. But worst of all was that on the white-painted finger was a ring with a large opal sitting in an elaborate silver setting. Franz's ring. Her husband's ring. Unmistakeable.

Frightened and upset by the choking noises her mother was making, Lisel pointed to the table and sang: "Look, Mama. Look! It's Papa. Papa's come back!"

The First Hours Of The Full Moon

Chihiro had caught the bus to visit her sister. At least that was what she had told everyone. But she knew she wouldn't be seeing her, so she thought she'd best ring her soon to ensure there was some news to tell everyone. She had felt a pang of guilt at the bus station but that soon became lost in the clouds of summer dust rising from the road as she left the city behind.

The inn was 20 miles north of the city; traditional enough to be comfortable, but desperate enough for customers, situated as it was on such a quiet road, to be discreet.

They met just once every year. A coded note through the post a few days in advance of the arranged date was all the contact she had with him. She knew his name was Toshio and that was all she wanted to know. She imagined he was a salaryman in the city but she chose not to find out and forced herself not to care.

After almost 20 minutes, the bus dropped her at the side of the road, seemingly in the middle of nowhere. She stood patiently for a short while and then became bored and started to look around. For the first time she noticed that the city was almost visible between the distant hills; maybe on a clear day, at least, but now there was too much haze.

The shade allowed by a stand of trees enticed her to walk a short distance. Finally she saw a big blue car driving towards her. Was this him? The car was different but maybe he'd changed it since last year.

The car drew level and stopped alongside her. She dared to bend to look inside and almost didn't recognise him through the windscreen; his hair had changed and he was wearing dark glasses. She got in and smiled at him.

He nodded to her and they exchanged one or two pointless pleasantries but did not touch.

It was late afternoon by the time they reached the inn. She stood back and allowed him to go through the usual formalities with the proprietress. As she waited she couldn't help noticing that the flowers in the vase in the hallway were dead; it looked as though they had been for some time.

She followed him in silence, staring at his back and wondering why he still wanted to meet her after all this time. She had been young when they had first met and recognised something in each other. Now her breasts and buttocks had sagged as she'd watched her thighs grow fat and her belly slacken. The last thing she was going to do was to question his motives or try to guess what they might be. All she knew was that this one day was what kept her living her grey, disordered life back in the city; she loathed this day and desired it in equal measure.

As the afternoon softened into evening, the light faded and darkness crept around the inn, making it feel even more isolated. They ate a quick meal in their room before attempting to speak to each other. They fell into silence, sitting and looking at one other, before Chihiro broke the stillness by announcing she was going to the bathroom.

When she returned, he tried to sit her down and talk to her but she turned away. "I don't want to know anything."

"But you've got to listen to me."

Why now, after all this time? She didn't want to know him or anything about him. He eventually gave up after a short while but then she was afraid the silence would last too long.

Finally, he came to her and began to undress her, pulling her this way and that and swearing softly to himself. Making sure that he didn't see, she allowed herself to smile.

Once her clothes lay at her feet, he slipped a length of rope out of his jacket pocket and grabbed her wrists, tying them quickly behind her. She stood wearing just her bra and his rope but somehow she still felt overdressed.

She moaned as he hauled her up and carried her to the bed, dumping her unceremoniously across it like a sack of provisions. His hands on her body felt like soft electricity, awakening her skin and her senses.

She stared up at the dark sky through the open window. The full moon had just come up and she felt as though it was smiling plumply down at her, head on one side, wishing like her that this night would outlast its allotted time. The night seemed to invade her mind, filling it with a darkness that hid the forbidden joys she craved.

He finally retrieved her from where he had laid her and hauled her up over his shoulder. There was no way that Chihiro could deny that she belonged to him, was his to do with as he pleased; the thought pleased her immeasurably.

Toshio placed her in a chair. Her head span as he pressed his mouth down onto the softest part of her flesh. She strained towards pleasure; so close yet denied to her until he was ready to grant it.

He knotted a handkerchief and slipped it between her teeth, tying it at the back of her head. She knew what was next and her pulse started to race. He lifted her up then laid her across his knees. The first smack landed on her left buttock and she yelped with surprise.

She began to melt inside as a stinging warmth spread across her flesh. Her mind raced as her breathing became faster.

Chihiro sank into a special place where she felt owned and protected and cared for. It was a place she could only enter when she was here with him.

After several moments she realised that he was talking, a rambling monologue that was interspersed with sobs. She felt several hot tears splash onto her buttocks, alternated with stinging blows. She closed her eyes tightly and tried not to listen to him as he poured out his pain to her. Chihiro knew she shouldn't hear this and couldn't help him even if she did; his humiliations and defeats were none of her business.

His cheeks were still wet when he'd finished hitting her and pulled her to her feet in front of him. He slapped her once across the face, pushing her back onto the bed. Within seconds he was holding her down and forcing his way inside her roughly. Chihiro was overwhelmed with animal joy, her mind and body dissolving in a blur of sweat and pain and happiness.

*

Chihiro began to feel cold. The sweat had cooled on her body some time ago but her lover had left her naked, uncovered, as he lay and watched her.

Finally he rose from the bed and fumbled in his pocket. Even though it was dark, she knew what it was and heard the slight metallic sound as he unsheathed it.

He knelt on the bed and showed her the blade. He didn't need to say anything as he rolled her over so that she lay on her face.

Toshio ran his hand along the back of her right thigh until, just below her buttock, he found what he was looking for, barely discernible beneath his fingers. He ran his fingers gently over the two rows of short scars; there were 19 in all, one for each year they had met in this place.

Quickly he pushed the blade against her skin. He could tell that she was holding her breath, waiting. Suddenly he drew the blade quickly across the skin, making her gasp behind the gag. He watched as a small ruby of blood eased its way from between the separated skin before he knelt and kissed it away.

Chihiro whimpered slightly as he rolled her over and undid the gag. He held her to him, crushing her in his arms. Finally they slept, entwined.

*

The next morning was quiet, both inside and outside their room. After a simple breakfast, he paid the bill and drove her down to the main road where she would catch her bus home.

They said goodbye and promised to meet again the following year. They hadn't kissed once. He looked sad as she closed the door and walked away.

The walk to the bus stop was a short one. Yet it was still long enough for Chihiro to replay the night's events in her mind. Afterwards, she felt like a flower that blossomed just once every year.

On the bus ride home, Chihiro couldn't help smiling to herself. The sweet pain on the back of her thigh reminded her that, after 20 long years, he still loved her even if her husband did not.

Bitterbloom

Now there was nowhere left for her to run. She could feel the cold brick through the thin cotton of her dress as her breath hiccuped roughly into her sore lungs and the sweat began to dry on her body. It felt like she'd been running for 100 years.

He'd be here any minute now. He couldn't be far behind her. She reached down and tugged at the flower from home pinned to the front of her dress; that's how he'd known what she was. How the hell could she have been so stupid to think that she wouldn't run into a collector tonight? When Jassy had given it to her just before she'd left to return home, she couldn't have guessed how stupid her sister would be.

She could hear boots crunching at the end of the alley. She panted, looking up into the rain-heavy sky visible between the narrow walls. If only she'd run out into the street, into the open, instead of simply hoping the shadows at the back of the club would swallow her.

He was standing there, she knew, and she didn't dare lower her eyes. Maybe it would be best if she didn't see it coming. But he would make her look at him, make her bow before him, that was the only certainty now.

She clenched her eyes shut tightly and lowered her head. Tiny drops of rain began to fall on her face. His footsteps drew nearer and she could hear his breathing gradually returning to normal after his exertions.

Finally he was only a few steps away. "There's no need to be frightened, my dear. I'll be very gentle. It's your destiny, you know."

At the sound of his voice, she began to sob quietly. She couldn't help herself, even though she desperately didn't want to appear weak before him; that would make it worse. She'd wanted to have a child with the right man and now it was over; her one chance gone. She had no more life left to live after tonight, the next few minutes.

She felt him press closer to her and then jumped as she felt his hand on her thigh. It was hot and moist. He pressed into her soft skin and moved his hand further up her thigh, lifting her dress as he did so.

"Look at me," he ordered. She sobbed softly for a few seconds, then forced her eyes to open and stay open. He was huge and hideous, with sunken eyes and a fat face below a smooth forehead. He tried to smile and she felt more afraid than she ever had before. "I won't hurt you," he reassured her. He smelt of expensive perfume.

Then his hand moved and he pulled the material to one side as he reached forward. "N-no, no, nononono," she began to whimper. He ignored her and sent his fingers straight to the sensitive spot at the top of her hot cleft.

He began to work on her, intent on bringing her to the peak of her pleasure as quickly as possible.

His fingers were almost like those of a woman, delicate and precise in their movements. The contrast between his bulk and gentleness shocked her and she wished he'd be as brutal as she thought he would be. At least that way surrendering to him might seem as dirty as it should be; that wouldn't seem so bad.

He began to speed up, making gentle circles around her clitoris with a swift urgency. He listened to her breath panting from between her parted lips, an edge of desperation becoming more apparent every second. After several more minutes the girl let out a squeal and her legs began to shudder as she surrendered to her orgasm.

He held her there, waiting for her ringing senses to calm themselves.

As she moaned and sagged forward, he caught her in one

enormous arm. He purred at her: "Give it to me now, baby. C'mon. Don't hold back. I've earned it, haven't I?"

Within seconds, the top of her head seemed to fold downwards, parting giant petals of flesh and soft bone. Cranial juice and blood dripped over her face and her breathing grew shallow as he watched with wonder, hardly daring to breathe on her.

From inside sprang slowly a red and blue protuberance, a giant fleshy flower that opened immediately on seeing the light. And there, sat at the exact centre, was what he'd come so far to find.

Holding her carefully in his left arm, he reached over with his right and delicately plucked the black, pearl-like object from its resting place. He let her body slide to the floor as her breathing stuttered, then stopped altogether.

He looked at the delicacy. He'd chased rumours across two planets to find this morsel. He'd heard of these women since he was a young man and, for so long, didn't believe they were real. But when he'd seen filmed evidence of their existence, it had become his obsession.

No money seemed able to purchase one of the Carellian bitterblooms, and in any case this was a task to savour in person, rather than trust to some hired help. Which was why he had come in person.

He put out his tongue and touched it. There was a slight tingling sensation and then he put it between his teeth and bit down swiftly. He chewed a small part of it, letting it slide over his tongue and down his throat, before popping the whole thing in his mouth.

"Mmmmmm. Delicious. So sweet, so succulent," he murmured to himself, delicately wiping the corners of his mouth. His face wore a look of complete satisfaction, unlike any other he'd known before, as he walked away from the slumped corpse of the girl in the filthy back alley.

A Million Miles Of Rain

He dreamed of a dog on a piece of high land, overlooking the sea. When he woke the dog was long dead and the sea was a million or more miles away, and probably as dry as a desert by now.

But this was the driest of places. The nearest river was at least 60 miles away and the last ocean that flowed here was merely a geological echo, a memory set in stone far below the dust.

The sea had once been his whole life, until an unravelling, uncontrolled line had taken his foot off. No skipper had any use for a man with a wooden foot. If you can't keep your balance on a pitching deck then you're just dead weight on a boat; ballast.

Sometimes he was sure he could feel it still, a phantom foot living inside the wood, wiggling its toes, the itch between them demanding to be scratched. Imagination was a minor curse, however.

The few women he'd spent time with since his accident, sweating over him with their hungry mouths and hungrier vaginas, had convinced him the accident had taken more from him than his foot.

Once he'd loved the sea but he now looked out with bitterness at the waves, beasts too big and too wild to face. It was then that he came to this place, thinking it as far from the shoreline as a man with his Ahab-like impediment could get.

The heat in this old shack was an enemy, too. It threatened to melt him while he slept and allowed him no rest during the baking days, so that he felt tired and drained every hour of the day and night.

After months (though it seemed like years) of dry, crackling summer there was heaviness in the air. The rain was coming. It hadn't abandoned him, after all.

One day, about a year ago, he'd been caught in a storm. He'd struggled homeward against the hard driving raindrops as they stung his face.

Then, as a rush of fire filled him, he realised what was happening to him and had struggled out of his wet, clinging clothes as quickly as he could.

Standing at the edge of the field, he'd yelled in exultation, as the rain washed over him and bounced off his body in a shining penumbra, blinking down at the erection standing out from his lower belly.

Biting off chunks of air and forcing them down, he'd felt whole for the first time in over three years. He'd cried as the rain had washed away the sticky droplet emerging from the tip of his hard penis.

He'd believed that fast running water, a distant echo of his old love, the sea, was his salvation.

He'd tried standing under a shower once he'd discovered the secret that unlocked his manhood. But the predictable flow of water merely washed him clean, leaving him unaroused and flaccid. If he was able to predict how the water would caress him, he was lost.

But nature was an unpredictable mistress. He could not guess whether she would hurl hail at him, whipping his skin with heavy pellets of fast stinging ice, or if instead he would be touched by the finest misty drizzle, like the merest of careless kisses.

That was when he knew the rain was his only lover.

The shack was hot, as usual, and he lay across the bed trying to breath or move or think. When he took a breath it was as thick as soup and tasted of salt and heat.

Suddenly the roof of the shack began to vibrate and complain as it suffered the a barrage of blows from above. It was here. The rain had come for him at last. The cacophony rose second by second.

He stripped off his clothes and flung open the door. The ground in front of the shack was being beaten and churned into mud by the impatience of the downpour.

Sticking his head out, he felt the water drumming on the back of his skull, tapping out the morse of its arrival. Then he stepped outside and felt his body stung and tickled and whipped and anointed by the blessed balm.

The sky above was dark, assuring him that the rain would not stop soon. He took a few steps forward, his body shivering with the chill of desire.

He looked down. There it was. His erection strained free of its skin sheath, moving with the pulse of his life as it flowed to the very end. He looked up, opened his mouth to drink, and smiled.

Wanting to be out on the open earth, away from the creaking, complaining shack, he began to run. A dog ran past him, barking in annoyance and looking for cover. He pitied the dog for not knowing the joy he knew.

He ran on, his foot becoming anchored in the mud, the stump sucked free of the wooden cup by his onward momentum. For seconds his leg flailed in the air as he hopped forward. He'd never tried to walk on just the ruined end of his leg and he was afraid of using the phantom foot that would not hold him up.

Panting and hopping, he pitched forward into the mud, spattered with dirt.

As he hit the ground, lightning flashed, either in the sky or in his head, and he pressed himself against the earth, convulsing, gasping, letting his semen leak into the mud.

Electricity and water met in him now, flashing and crackling, threatening to split him apart in their mutual fury.

With the dirt beneath his cheeks, his breath rasping out of him, his mouth filling with rain, a dream filled his mind. Huge planes of grey-green held him, slid beneath him, bucked and then fell away. He was alone at sea, whole again, perfect again; it filled his heart and he saw himself sailing a vessel built only for him, designed to set him free.

The waves ran high above him and crashed in a tingling spray over his naked body, fire and lust filling every tense muscle, yet didn't upend the boat. It seemed too big to be a dream, it wanted to rush out his skull as if it was something real, something he knew to be true.

Lying panting, pressed against the ground, he knew what he must do.

Struggling to his knees, dripping with mud and his own seed, he looked behind him. His foot was sticking out of the grey mush like a grounded derelict.

Turning, he headed back to it on all fours. After retrieving it, he would go and wash, then dress. He decided he would rest to build up his strength before setting off; there was a million miles of rain between him and the ocean.

Karas d'carcasse

"Stay here, Sergeant. I won't be long." Major Calloway swung his feet out of the jeep. As he walked up the steps of the hospital, he looked up; the sky was heavy with snow.

The place was the biggest children's hospital in Vienna and was still struggling to cope with the after-effects of the war. Too many sick children and not enough drugs to go round. As he opened the door, the stuffy heat almost knocked him over.

He took off his beret, loosened his coat and asked the receptionist to call Dr Winkel.

As soon as the doctor arrived, he led the Major to a ward that lay down a long corridor. The Major knew full well the reason for its isolated position; it was a ward where the patients had no expectation of recovery. He'd been here before.

As soon as he entered, he recognised a smell that was only too familiar to him from the battlefield. He swallowed hard and followed the doctor to a cot near the door.

The doctor pulled back the screen and indicated the cot. Calloway looked for just a second, then sucked in his breath sharply. It was several seconds before he dared let it out again.

This one was much worse than the others the doctor had shown him in the past. "Good God!!"

"If He's got anything to do with it, He should be bloody well ashamed," muttered the doctor.

Calloway struggled to retain his professional composure. "S-so ... Doctor, tell me ... what caused this."

"More infected penicillin, I'm afraid, Major. A fresh batch in yesterday. We thought it was good until we used

it. It's been 'cut' with something."
"'Cut'? With what?"
"I don't know. And neither does anyone else here - we've not seen anything like it before." The doctor reached into his pocket and took out a piece of paper. Calloway looked at it. It was some sort of formula - it meant nothing to him. He handed it back quickly.

"Is it something the Nazis cooked up in one of their damned camps?" Calloway's brusqueness betrayed his intense dislike of mysteries.

The doctor could almost see impatience rising from the Major like steam. "I don't know, I'm sorry. There's just no way of knowing."

Calloway grunted and cast his gaze around the ward. It was filled with screened-off cots, all of them occupied. The doctor had referred to them as children, but Calloway struggled to think of them like that. The breathing thing on the mattress turned its eyes to him but he couldn't meet its gaze.

"We think we know where the stuff is coming from, anyway." The Major felt he should offer some small scrap of hope in this hopeless place.

"Yes?"

"A black marketeer called Karas. He appeared in Vienna about two months ago; gave the Russians the slip and ended up on our doorstep, unfortunately. He's a French-Hungarian emigre, as far as we can make out ... though the paper trail is thin. Unsurprising, given how much was destroyed in the war."

The doctor looked skeptical. "Don't worry, doctor, we'll get him. The noose is tightening all the time," lied Calloway, knowing full well that Karas could melt between the Russian and British zones at will.

A quick trip to the morgue, where the doctor showed him the stomach-churning final result of the 'penicillin', only served to heighten Calloway's resolve to trap the filthy little racketeer who exchanged money for young lives.

*

The translation was bad; it had been done by the Russians. Though it was clear even from their wrecked English that they believed the man they referred to in their equally bad French as 'Karas d'carcasse' was now dead.

Calloway picked up the photograph of the man's body. Unidentifiable, as you'd expect of anyone who'd fallen from the top of the Wiener Riesenrad wheel in the Prater amusement park.

The report said that the wheel's operator had stopped the contraption in order to let some people off. That's when he saw the body fall. Several fellow passengers identified the corpse as being that of Karas.

When he'd received the report last month, Calloway had been struck by the coincidence of somebody who knew Karas actually being there at the time. Except if they'd been the one to push him, of course.

The Russians hadn't held them, or even bothered to identify them properly. They were probably just glad that Karas was out of their hair; a corpse wouldn't bother them any more.

But whoever had died falling from the park amusement ride, it wasn't Karas. Calloway was sure of that after what he'd seen tonight.

*

Calloway stopped off for a whisky or two at what passed for the officer's club on his way to his quarters. The place was nearly empty and nobody bothered him. He sat in the corner and tried to drown the image of the child on the bed. What he'd seen in the war was bad enough; why did he have to put up with this as well? He didn't need any further proof that the world was as rotten as month-old meat; certainly not from a professional misery-monger like Karas. And what sort of twisted bastard was the man anyway?

Once in bed, anaesthetised by the spirits in his stomach, Calloway slid quickly into an uneasy sleep.

He dreamed of a man, huge and hunched forward strangely. He stood atop a giant wheel. It was night.

After some moments, he stood bolt upright and shouted his defiance at Calloway. Then he lifted his arms to the sky and tore at it with his hands. Holes began to appear, showing an even darker blackness behind the cloak of night, from which a vile poison began to drip onto the ground below, wizening everything it touched.

The blackness began to seep into the ground, making it boil, and spread towards where Calloway stood. He tried to lift his feet to step back; he needed to retreat from the foul contagion. But he was stuck. He pulled and pulled, but he was stuck. The black stain was almost at his shoes.

Then suddenly he found himself swimming through filth, muck, bits of rubbish, as if in an enormous sewer. As he began to feel himself drown, Calloway woke, sweating and panting heavily. He reached for the glass of water on the table by his bed. As he lifted it to his lips, he saw the surface was covered in a layer of dust.

*

He must have fallen back to sleep, because he was awoken by the telephone ringing.

On the other end were the disinterested tones of his driver, Sergeant Paine. "I thought you'd like to know, sir. They've

Karas d'carcasse

tracked down Karas."

Calloway was halfway into his clothes, telling Paine to bring the jeep round at once. He was already standing on the roadside waiting when Paine careered round the corner. The jeep had barely slowed down before Calloway was in the passenger seat and they were speeding off again.

Still half-awake despite the chill air, Calloway forced a question out of his numb mouth. "How did we find out about him, Paine?"

"A tip-off, sir. A woman called Anna phoned, said she used to be his girlfriend. Turns out her sister's boy was taken into hospital with appendicitis. After the op, they gave him some of Karas's penicillin. You can imagine the results, sir."

"Yes, I can," muttered Calloway. Though, in truth, he was trying hard not to imagine it.

Sergeant Paine swung the jeep around a corner sharply, narrowly missing a pile of rubble that spilled across the darkened street. Overhead, the stars shone down coldly on the evidence of man's stupidity. Ahead Calloway could see a knot of three British soldiers standing around something on the floor. The jeep lurched to a halt and Calloway jumped out, boots clicking efficiently on the wet roadway.

As he approached, a corporal came towards him. "Hello, sir. I think he was trying to reach the sewer, sir, when we got him."

Calloway nodded. "That's where he belongs." He walked over to the body slumped forward on the wet cobbles.

"It isn't pretty, sir," said the Corporal.

Calloway glanced over his shoulder at the man. "I've no doubt ..." Carefully he turned the body over with his foot. The corpse's blood-stained coat opened to reveal the true face of the man who'd caused so much suffering.

Like the children in the hospital, the body had too many faces and limbs. Small, half-formed arms the colour of something seen in a butcher's shop window reached towards Calloway. Three of Karas's eyes were still open. Under other circumstances, the Major would have reached down to close them.

But the thing lying before him didn't deserve compassion. Not only because of what Karas had done, but because Calloway wasn't entirely sure he was human. Anymore.

He stood and walked towards his jeep. "Burn the body. For God's sake, burn it ..."

"But, sir ..."

"Burn it!!"

*

Back in his office, Calloway pawed at the paperwork to do with the case. It was all nonsense and he knew it. Eventually he shut off the light, saluted the duty sergeant at the front desk and stepped out into the bitter Viennese night. At the margins of the street lighting, piles of rubble disappeared into the darkness. A light snow had begun to frost the ruins.

As he walked to the bar he usually frequented, he mused that Karas had made the unforgiveable error of any drug dealer - he'd become a user. Then he thought of the man's corpse and wondered if anyone could ever choose that?

Maybe after all he was used and not a user, thought the Major. The city was filled with thousands of victims - at best, misunderstood, at worst, despised - and perhaps Karas was just one of them. If so, whatever it was that had used Karas, had no place in this world, he thought. But it was still there, he knew, waiting out in the darkened ruins of the city, shielded from view by the slow falling snowflakes.

Wunderkind

Here they are again, the curiosity seekers. And here am I, a curiosity to be sought.

In this wood-lined room in a back-of-beyond University town, my 'owner', my 'keeper', sees fit to display me to so-called medical students and their shrivelled-souled friends.

You will always find me here; his born-but-never-born bi-cranial bitch; a four-eyed freak floating in formaldehyde.

Von Bilt. He'll tell anyone who'll listen that he's a specialist. But merely in trickery and take-the-mickery, as far as I can see. His only qualifications or credentials are locked away behind the doors of these glass-fronted cabinets.

Undoubtedly his offer to help my suffering mother was nothing more than a gambit to get at me, the beast within her belly. She died on the operating table, having never seen me. So perhaps it was all for the best.

No doubt his curiosity got the better of him. And us.

I never even got to draw one single breath - 'complications' was the official explanation - before I found myself here; alive but oh-so-dead.

Sound penetrates through the discoloured liquid to my submerged mind. "Two heads are better than one, they say. Hahahahah!" Oaf after oaf has entertained his friends with this witty epithet as they stare at my helpless, naked body floating before them.

Only I am really qualified to comment on that remark and I can affirm that the answer is in the negative. One head, containing one fully-formed brain, is more than enough for anyone; yet so many wander the world without one, like some Oz-bound scarecrow.

These staring sheep. Can't they see how alive and alone I am? Or perhaps they simply don't care.

There are others in this room. Across the way from me, in similar glass-fronted cabinets, more of my kind dwell in this vile place. The nearly made and the badly finished; deformed, preserved, gawped at. From my liquid tomb, my vile womb of glass, it is impossible to tell if they share my torment. They may be alive like me, yet frozen in their moment - long gone - of desuetude and death.

Von Bilt, with his self-satisfied smirk and his stiff-coated stance, lords it over us all. His blood lubricates my dreams.

In my freest fantasies, we can talk to each other, we bottled things. We whisper and we plot and we connive.

And one evening I imagine we contrive to call him back to our happy home after dark, on some pretext or other, and that we step from our prisons, passing through the glass as if it were fog. When the shadows come out to play.

We surround him in a disjointed dance, like an obscenely coreographed ossuary, our discoloured bodies limping towards him from every side and surrounding him, overpowering him.

First I would flip open his cranium and scoop out the voltaic jelly that hides behind those cold eyes, plopping it into a bowl where it could slowly lose its charge. Nothing too quick; that'd be too good for him. I want him to know what's happening to him, in the same way I've 'known' all these years.

And then we would take him to pieces. Bright baubles of ruby-hued flesh flying through the air to land in their own preserving jars, stacked away on shelves and put on show daily to gawkers galore.

Until von Bilt would be measured out in meat; carefully stored, bit by bit, so that we would know where every last cruel morsel of him sat, his painful demise perfectly preserved. A flawless mirror, in fact, of our own agonies.

Of course there will be one thing missing - his seeping sewer of a soul no doubt fled the scene of the crime years ago

Sustenance

It happens twice a day (whatever a day is). Everything happens twice a day; he is allowed to sleep twice a day, he is fed twice a day, he can relieve himself twice a day.

And, twice a day, he creates food for his people.

He sits on the edge of his bed and looks up at the thing on the wall. He cannot know what it says because he cannot read ... or can no longer read. But it changes at regular intervals and he knows it somehow marks the way time moves on, passes by. Though all time is the same to him now.

The grey walls are empty apart from the device. The floor is empty apart from his bed, his chair and his table. And then there is the barrier. It rises nearly to his waist and prevents him from climbing into the place where the water is. But he can see through it.

He hates the water because he knows the water is why he is how he is. Here, on the lower levels of the city, rivers or ponds or streams are miles and miles above him. And all filled with poison. Yet there is water here.

*

He sits at his solitary table and stirs the brownish paste with his spoon, knowing it must be full of chemicals, drugs to make him compliant and to maintain his genetic 'gift'. But what choice does he have? He needs sustenance. One man's poisson is another man's poison, he thinks and giggles to himself for a moment. He doesn't like the sound, finding it strange and painful, and stops suddenly. He wonders where the curious phrase came from.

Sustenance

Once he had refused to eat. For three days he had pushed away the plate of vaguely flavoured savoury mush they provided him with. Then they took him and did something to him. He can't remember what; he struggles to remember anything at all now.

He was foolish to defy them, they told him. He does remember them saying that. After all, what were the desires of one man against the crushing needs of billions of hungry mouths?

He still has memories, but they are all mis-shapen and he fears they may only be dreams. Yes, he's sure he has memories - some sort of memories, at least - of a childhood spent in the filth-strewn streets on the surface; dodging among the mountains of detritus between home and school, face masked against the stench. But that was a million years ago, or more.

There had been some sort of deal involving his parents; there must have been. That's when they would have taken him and changed him. Forever.

And now he is a feeder.

*

When the siren sounds, he has a few moments to rid himself of the grey overall and to kneel, naked, on the floor near the barrier. Then he closes his eyes and waits.

Soon the steam begins to pour in from vents near the top of the walls. It is heavy and, as it fills the room with its stifling whiteness, he struggles to breathe. His scrawny frame becomes hot and sweaty.

If he could stop himself sweating, he would. It is his greatest wish and his most persistent dream; a world without sweat. He thinks of it always as he kneels, shaking, sweat pouring from his cave-fish skin.

Sustenance

It drops onto the floor and runs down the gentle incline, through the narrow gap at the bottom of the barrier and into the water. In the middle of each bead is a tiny shape, silvery-black, wriggling and moving. Once in the water, the tiny shapes dart around, tasting their freedom. How he envies them.

When the steam stops, he remains kneeling for a while, waiting for the sweating to stop. The room soon grows cold and he collapses on his side, gasping and moaning. He crawls over to the barrier and gazes into the water as his thousands of 'children' swim around.

They grow before his eyes, becoming a few inches long within a matter of minutes. Only then do the sluice gates open and all the water drains away, taking the tiny fish with them. He always feels sorry to see them go. Even though he hates what he has become, he still feels they are his and that nobody else has a right to them.

He struggles to feel a sense of pride that he, along with hundreds of others, is providing sustenance for his people. But all he feels is pained and despairing and old before his time.

*

The bare wall faces him. Often he dreams that he wakes and the walls have all crumbled while he slept. Yet he never dreams what is beyond them - it is all just darkness, and an ominous rushing sound that seems to draw nearer and nearer yet never arrives.

High up near the top of the wall is a small door with a window set into it. It is way out of reach even if he stood on the table. The door is what they use if they ever need to enter this place.

Sometimes there is a small face at the window. She looks down at him as if she remembers him from somewhere else.

Sustenance

Her eyes are filled with pain and pity. But then the siren always sounds and she is gone. He is never allowed to get as far as wondering who she is.

*

As he sits at his table, doing nothing, weighed down by despair, it comes to him. A single thought like a light coming on in a room too long in darkness.

He stands and looks down at the chair on which he has been sitting. His hands slide along the back and he tests its weight by lifting it from the floor. Even though the numbers are meaningless to him, the thing on the wall tells him the siren will sound soon, when the black marks move to a certain place.

He waits, hands gripping and back tensed ready. Then, as the siren sounds, he heaves the chair above his head and swings it down against the barrier. The material shatters and slides down under the surface of the water, becoming almost invisible.

Almost at once, he hears clattering sounds coming from behind the walls as feet scurry here and there.

As the steam begins to pour into the room, he climbs carefully down into the water. It is cold and it feels so odd to him, making him shiver as he wades forward. He is afraid of it, but not so afraid that he climbs back out. Better this than the life he has.

The steam is filling the room now but he is too cold to sweat. It feels wonderful: this is his dream.

He hears the door in the wall open and there are voices mingled with the steam. But the vapour cloaks him as he wades to the far wall.

His head slips below the water as he lies back, causing only a slight wave. Looking up through the liquid and the clearing steam, he can see the monotonous grey roof of his cell, broken only by two weak lights set into the ceiling.

He closes his eyes slowly and prepares to breathe in the darkness.

All The Fun Of The Unfair

With a cast iron wife as cold as old tripe, Blatch often tried to reach into his past in search of a warm kiss or two.

Triumphant rust has crawled across her face, blotching her one eye and completely obscuring her soul. Each evening, on his return from the dust works, he would sit in their cramped house, head turned to one side, gazing into distant dead days.

There was a time ... . Yes, there had been a time when he was young and had been loved. He remembered her face so well. And the park where they would meet under the drooping trees.

He could remember the place well enough but not her name. His mind was like the oldest machines at the factory; creaking and groaning, working only intermittently. Who was she? And where was she in time?

Dimly, achingly it came to him, swimming through the murk of his memory. That summer now long lost struggled to the scummy surface. Yet still no name. Ah, well.

It would require a feat of inner strength, a victory of the imagination, but Blatch knew he could do it. If he wired his memory into the yearning machinery of his heartache, he could provide enough power, he knew it. He'd go back. Back ... and never come forth again!

Her smile. Her face. Those perfect, symmetrical kisses, full of hot breath, tobacco-scented yet minty clean. That was what he wanted. All of it.

One soulless Sunday, he sat. In the broken glasshouse in the overgrown garden, he could get some peace. He screwed up his face and his stomach in concentration.

If he could focus on where they first met. But after some moments, he remembered that he'd forgotten ... years before. "Damn! I have no excuse for my own excuses," he mused.

But he did know what town it was. He remembered that, at least.

He sat and strained his soul and memory. Bright flashes of nothing burst in his head. He would go back now, he could feel it. The small squares, leaning clock towers and wide marshes of Felompsy were within his grasp, if not yet under his feet. "Come on. Come on."

Then he felt as if he was floating. Just a little more effort, he told himself. That's it! The darkness began to clear but only a little. He became aware of an overwhelming odour of a very human sort.

Something wet and unpleasant slid under his feet and he put out a hand to steady himself. Then it struck him like a rubber mallet in the face. That was why the gloom wasn't clearing - he was underground. He arrived in the ancient sewers that drained into the seaward marshes.

He held his nose and edged forward. If he could find a ladder ...

Blatch had spent many a happy childhood hour in these very sewers with his fellow 'rat boys'. And there was always a special prize at the end of the day for anyone who found anything dead. Anything, at all.

Once he'd found a dead soul, limp and filmy and flimsy, lying on a low ledge. But his only prize had been a greasy, hobnailed kicking from the departed's loitering relatives.

"Ah yes," Blatch sighed, thinking that his sense of smell must have been less well-developed in those days.

Finally he exited the stench and clinging memories by way of a fortuitous ladder and grating. He climbed out stiffly and was pleased to see he was in the right street. His memory was serving him well now, he thought, as he clapped his hands together. And the weather was playing along, too.

Squelching forward in his stool-stained slippers, he was delighted to see that he'd arrived in that vermilion July way-back-when. "When? When things were better, that's when! When things were younger and so was I ... "

He laughed, almost danced, feeling like a child again, as the onion-scented armpit of Summer welcomed him back.

The haunted fairground, filled with chuckles and pink delights, stood before him. That was where she was waiting, he now knew, and imagined her flying high on one of the more delicious rides, excited and filled with love. For him, he hoped. For him, again.

He padded wetly through the entrance arch of bone, spit and cardboard, fashioned in the shape of a gaping whale's mouth. Phantoms of happiness and desire, loud and brightly painted, crowded around and ahead of him. But Blatch knew he had to ignore them, press on, find her. He knew she was here.

Pink delights and sweet pickled laughs jostled him here and there, pushed him back and forth, tugged him to and fro. But he kept his eyes peeled and his feet firmly planted in his soggy slippers.

Finally, he saw her standing by the Brandy Floss stall. His heart nearly stopped rotating when he saw her face, so pale and so perfect, lit by the afternoon sun. The sky seemed greener, the grass bluer, and he felt so young again, so filled with love for her.

Then he noticed that she was talking to a Sky Sailor with huge metals wings folded across his back. And she was laughing.

Squelching closer, Blatch could hear him brag: "Oh yes, we go quite high you know ... quite a long, long way up. I even stroked the moon once." This wasn't the way he remembered it.

No, this wasn't how it was. She'd been alone, he was certain. Alone. Until he came along. He wriggled his fingers through the tottering piles of old memories. Things scittered here and there, seeking to evade his unpleasantly probing digits, until finally he gave up with a heavy sigh of resignation.

It was time to intervene. Yes, that was the only answer. He'd force things to be the way they were. He wasn't going to let time trick him out of his prize. And nobody was going to steal his perfect summer, his sweetest love.

Blatch dashed forward and grasped the pompous sky sailor around the knees, bringing him down. The man partly recovered and started clawing at Blatch's face. For minutes they rolled in the earth and the Earth rolled under them.

A small group of spectators gathered, while others yelped and ran off to pursue their own fancies.

A bout of eye gouging and testicle tugging ensued, leaving them both sore and exhausted, until finally Blatch flipped himself round and trod on the man's head. The uniformed figure under Blatch's boot lay still. Chuckling to himself, Blatch had no time to enjoy his glorious victory as he was lifted bodily from atop his trophy.

The woman of his dreams had him by his collar and was dangling him off the ground. "Blatch! It is you, isn't it?"

He struggled to get his feet back on the ground and looked up into his beloved's face. 'Yes! yes, it is I ... I've come to find you. To save you. To love you!!"

Then, as he looked up at his beloved, he saw how she would change, how the years would alter her and ...

"You!" He let out a whimper of despair as he realised that she - his wonderful long-ago Summer sweetheart - and his wife - his hard-hearted stiff-backed grey jailer - were one and the same. And that time has eaten up his memories, chewed them over, sucking out all the juice, before spitting them out into the mud. "But I ... that is ... it isn't ... OooOoooh, no!"

The woman's fingers touched his cheek gently before lifting his chin. "Blatch, you fool. Did you think time would just stand still? Did you think we were immortal?"

Unimpressed by the braggart victor, the spectators had started to drift away.

Blatch blinked, large tears rolling down his chubby stubbled cheeks. "No. Well, that is .. I'd hoped .... things could ..." He sobbed. "I'd hoped for .... more."

The woman led Blatch to the bloodied figure of the Sky Sailor. "Look at him," she said, gently. "Don't you recognise him?" She bent down to flick a blob of mud from the elaborate brass insignia on the front of his uniform so that the tangle of wings and lightning bolts became clearly visible. Then she reached up to tug at an identical blemished badge worn by Blatch on the front of his grubby bath robe.

"Don't you even recognise yourself any more, Blatch?" She smiled at him sadly.

He didn't recognise himself, he now knew. It was true. He often wondered who that was in the mirror, imitating him as he shaved ... whenever he bothered to.

"I know you don't recognise me anymore," she said. "Perhaps you need new glasses."

His wife knelt by the figure lying in the dirt for a moment, then turned back to Blatch. "You'll live," she said and he chuckled with embarrassment.

She leaned forward and kissed his dirty, wrinkled brow. "You were a silly vain young man. I wasn't taken in for a minute," she said. "And you haven't got any better over the years. But I love you all the same. "

Blatch coughed, looked up at her and smiled. "I'm sorry."

She smiled back. "We won't go on forever, you know. Promise you'll be happy to die by my side, old fool?"

He nodded, realising he was too old for all this jumping

around in time. Especially on the evidence of the faulty clockwork of his memory. He took one last look around at his summer. The wind was colder than he'd remembered and, for a moment, the sun was obscured by the smoke from the crematoria at the edge of town.

"Home?"

"Home," he was forced to admit, as he lifted the iron sewer cover and began to climb inside.

Corpus Deliciosum

The late February wind. Arnold hated it. It always made him feel cold and old these days. But then he'd always felt old, even as a young man: always out of step with everyone around him.

He pulled his collar up and looked back at the big, ugly house. He'd intended to sell it when his last wife left, taking the two boys with her, but somehow he'd never got around to it. He disliked both the area and the people who lived here, but inaction had won out over his prejudices.

As he passed the street corner he noticed that there was a planning notice pinned to the lamp-post. Curious to find out what the interfering idiots at the local council were planning next, he stood and read it.

It said: 'Council Planning Notice: This is due notification that on March 15th of this year, Arnold Ernald will be torn down by court order. To be erected, in his place, will be a more noteworthy example of public-spirited humanity.'

Arnold could hear the blood rushing through his ears as his initial disbelief was replaced by anger. He stormed back inside his house, slamming the door hard behind him.

After several minutes on the telephone to his solicitor it became clear that the notice was legally binding. There was nothing he could do but submit. His previous emotions were now rudely elbowed out of the way by a feeling of black despair.

He couldn't understand what he'd done wrong. All he'd ever really wanted was to be left alone.

Arnold had come to the conclusion, too late, that there was no place in this world for someone as honest as him.

From his earliest years, his life had been a parade of bitterness, loss and betrayal. But he obviously wasn't allowed to show that outwardly; it wasn't what people wanted or expected. It more than likely upsets them, he thought.

Well, he had two weeks before he was to be 'torn down'. It was time enough to show them something they weren't expecting. If he had to go - and it seemed he did - then he would do it in his own way.

*

Pots boiled, vats bubbled, the sweetness started to seep and soon everything was changing.

*

On March 12th, everyone in the small community had an invitation, hand-delivered by courier, to a free 'Forgive And Forget Feast' at Arnold's house in three days' time.

At first people were suspicious - they didn't like Arnold and he'd made no secret of the fact that he hated them in turn. Many of them had smirked in satisfaction when the official notice announcing the old man's fate had been posted in the street. So why would he want to lay on a gastronomic extravaganza for them by way of a goodbye?

But concerned phone calls to Arnold's solicitor put their restless minds at ease. Yes, there was a specific clause in his will and, yes, the old man was already deceased (or soon would be).

Some stayed away out of petulance or fear, but most of those who had received the invitation turned up at the right time on the right day.

Even a casual observer passing by the line of people

gathered in the long hallway of Arnold's house would have noticed a greedy glint in each and every eye, the occasional tongue run over eager lips.

"This is the first time he's given anything to anyone for free," muttered a voice from the back of the line.

When the solicitor's clerk opened the large doors to the dining room at exactly 11 A.M., those who had gathered were faced with a large notice on a wooden stand. It said: 'Here lie the mortal remains of Arnold Ernald. Enjoy!'

Mouths gaped open and faces twitched uncomfortably as they saw what lay on the large table in front of them. Laid out in the centre, surrounded by place settings was the naked body of their former neighbour Arnold Ernald. But it wasn't as they had known him in life; it had undergone an unsettling transformation.

"I'm going! Even for him this is a sick joke. We're not cannibals, for God's sake," wailed a voice at the back as it faded into the distance.

Two of the boldest of the small crowd edged forward and leaned across the table. The man from across the road sniffed speculatively before whispering to himself "Sugar."

A tall, thin woman behind pushed him aside, nostrils twitching, and speculatively dug two sharp nails into the skin of the old man's stomach. She raised the thinnest of scrapings to her nose, sniffed deeply and suspiciously. Slowly a pink, questing tongue reached forward and licked the scrap of skin.

She laughed softly and nodded before plunging her fingers into the body once more. Emboldened by their own hunger, the others pushed forward, ignoring the cutlery and place settings.

They were all delighted with Arnold's novel surprise. All his petty cruelties and acid comments were forgotten as they tucked into his butterscotch brains and candied kidneys. They were prepared to believe that, when faced with stark reality, he'd had a change of heart (which was now, incidentally, a raspberry mousse).

The old man had plundered the secrets of Tibetan mystics, Indian mithai moguls, Native American shamans and Belgian chocolatiers to effect his marvellous metamorphosis. The final stages of the process had been overseen by a Voudou priest of Arnold's long acquaintance.

And he'd spent the last of his money persuading a number of trained medical technicians that their scruples weren't as deeply held as they'd previously believed them to be.

He had passed away the previous evening when the last of his blood had been drained away, to be replaced by a succulent, thick strawberry jelly.

The final sheen of sweat that had covered his dying body had now been transformed into a light dusting of delicious icing sugar.

The skin on which the sweat had dried had become a thin, crisp layer of pale toffee.

The venal grocer who lived three doors down made an outrageous cracking noise with his teeth as he burst open one of the old man's candyglow eyeballs to suck out the liquor within.

Arnold's slicksweet spleen shot the length of the table as it slurped out of the hands of the vicar's wife, only to be caught by the hand of and immediately stuffed into the mouth of the local plumber, whose pipes gurgled in delight.

The praline liver was a favourite with the elderly sisters whose dyspeptic Dalmatian had plagued Arnold's last years.

Ribs were ripped free and cracked open to reveal a succulent sticky centre inside the hard white candy, which tongues probed avidly and mouths sucked at noisily in order to extract every last drop of sugariness.

One mother broke off from her greedy guzzling just long enough to scoop his gobstopper testicles and lollipop penis from her children's hands, secreting the salacious items stickily in her pocket for later.

By the time they'd finished feasting, there was little left of Arnold except parts of the rum-and-raisin fudge spine and some penny chew toenails. Everyone drifted away with a full belly and a glad heart.

The bitter old man had ended his life in the sweetest way possible and would be remembered, at least for the next few minutes, with sticky, sugary lips and a series of soft belches.

It wasn't until the next day that the pains began ...

In An Ancient Embrace

Just as the sun is leaving, the wind chases them across the flattened, flooded fields - tripping over the half-submerged corpses of a gin-soaked couple - to his battered laboratory in the barracks district. They must succeed between bombardments.

Climbing over the rubble, he forces the door open with difficulty before helping her inside. They leave the sky behind as night begins to gather.

Gloved fingers brush fungal grey from the black diodes. Dials gaze upwards, hollow-eyed and blank-minded.

Brushing lank white hair away from his eyes, he glances about before muttering "It looks undamaged."

In the centre of the room is a large apparatus, covered by a filthy sheet. Grasping the material firmly, he pulls it free. The resulting dust cloud settles to reveal an enormous bronze head, its mouth hanging open. In place of its tongue sits a large black stone.

Although he designed the device to help the military command predict the outcome of battles with the help of the spirits, he is prepared to freelance from time to time, for the right price and motives. Today the device would be serving an entirely benign purpose, he assures himself.

He waves his arms at the object. "This remarkable device allows the user to intercept aetheric waves, resulting in -"

She allows him to ramble on, smiling and letting her attention wander. She hasn't sought explanations, only results. She had been a Countess, before things changed. Now all she wants to do is to find that which has been lost to her. A reunion is imperative in order to ease her empty, lonely heart.

Sensing her impatience, he hurries about his tasks; adjusting, re-calibrating, restoring. He needs this to work as much as she does - not that he truly cares about finding her 'lost one'. He thinks of the money she has offered and of how it will allow him to take his wife away from the fighting.

When the machine is ready, he approaches her. "You have the co-ordinates?"

She nods. "I have to tame my star," she lisps empathically. "Nothing in my life has shone as brightly." She twists her fingers into her silver furs, pulling them about her throat. Then, moving her small dog from one arm to the other, she hands him a slip of paper.

"The true vibrations of the Vorpal wind will grant us the result we desire, Madame. I can assure you of that."

Entering the digits, he realises the numbers indicate a location other than the surface of the Earth. Even though the numbers come from a noted Astronomer, he can't help feeling uneasy. He shrugs it off with some difficulty and continues - it won't be the first time he has intercepted the soul of a departed one trapped in the spaces between the worlds.

Electric arcs spark, electrons dance in the dark. Waves rise and fall, sounds converge, then diverge, in a symphony of interstellar emptiness.

The glass shard remnants of the shattered windows resonate to an ancient song as the black stone in the mouth of the device jumps to life, beginning to hum loudly.

She holds her breath as sounds begin to vibrate through the air. But what she hears is not what she longs for - the voice of a beast barking in a jungle far away, insane mathematics from the moon. They both recognise a radio broadcast - at least 40 years old - plucked from the space between the spheres and brought back down to Earth.

He senses her impatience, her disappointment. She fiddles

with her clothing, and hugs her protesting pet even closer, as if preparing to leave.

He scurries over to her. "Do not leave, madame! The words will come, the tongue will transmute the vibrations given time. Please -"

She prods the end of his nose with the tiniest morsel of affection and mutters, "You have one more chance." He grins, bows his head and turns back to the huge bronze head.

She sits for hours, her silver dog at her feet as she sips sweet wine, pulling her furs about her for the little warmth they provide.

He is on the verge of abandoning his task in despair, believing that the co-ordinates she gave him must be wrong. Or, impossibly, something is blocking the device. As the vibrations grow more intense, so does the cold. He can see his breath now and has to wipe frost from the dials.

The entire room begins to shake alarmingly. The small dog wakes, yelps, and bounds from the building in terror.

In the window frames, the tips of the glass fragments frost first. A sound bounces between the four walls, then hammers at the ceiling before dropping to the floor with a crash. It repeats and repeats.

This is no astral melody, but a chilling threnody. A dead star voice calling; dead starstuff leaking. It is a song she last heard in her father's observatory when still very small. It has been there forever and will be there forever still, cold and dead yet eternal. Now they will join as lovers, a binary eternity.

The cold is alarming yet still she shrugs off her furs. Tentacles of black ice snake into him, striking at his organs and stealing his breath.

Struggling to form thoughts, icing over instantly, he manages to command his freezing tongue. "Is this h-i-m - ?" His last thought struggles to grasp how any woman could possibly desire a lover who is so cold. As cold as her own madness.

Naked now, she stands erect, her blackening skin glistening with rime, spreading white, arms stretched to left and right like embryonic wings aching to ascend. "Yes ... Thanatos ... concealed by the Morbidiae Nebula ..."

Her tongue freezes to her teeth. His heart becomes ice in mid-beat. Their figures become transparent, near invisible, as the cold of the long-dead star fills the room before leaking out into the night that will last forever, all cross the frozen Earth.

Put On The Mask

Tickets for the performance can be found scattered all over town, though no-one dares pick them up for fear of becoming the supporting act. Not that there ever is one. Not in the way you or I would understand it, at least.

*

Lift the mask to your face, peering through the waiting eye holes. Put it on. Secure it in place. Wear it, uncertainly, uncomfortably, each day for the rest of your life. For fear that people see the truth in your face.

*

Motionless, he lies in the dream of days, unmoving and uncertain. But there is no rhythm of night and day for him, just endless grey. Since his accident, colour has been a thing only seen in memory and occasional dreams. Sounds increasingly hold less and less meaning.

He is aware of being the victim of something, if only of circumstance. Gathering his feeble energies, he concentrates on regaining the power of speech. But even that seems to be futile.

The doctor and two nurses who attend him, all masked, remain silent the whole time. One even refuses to answer questions, dismissing him with a slow shake of her head.

There is a clock on the wall opposite his bed. He makes careful note of the large black number in the date display. Whenever he is awake, he watches its slow progress as it crawls towards the top of its small window on the clock face. Only boredom and illness can provide the clarity needed to notice its tiny incremental movement.

Unaccountably, he awakes on the third day with his body healed. He feels healthy. There is no bruising and nothing is broken. His muscles don't ache in the least. His vision is clear and his hearing seems as sharp as it ever was. He knows he's been in some sort of accident but the details are missing.

At first he waits for the doctor or the nurses to appear. After an hour and a half he decides to rise from the bed. He dresses slowly in the clothes draped over the room's single chair, which he assumes are his, despite their unfamiliarity.

Poking his head out into the corridor, he sees no-one, so he walks down the corridor to the reception desk. Still there is no-one to be seen. After standing at the desk for five minutes watching another clock, expecting a nurse or receptionist to appear, he decides to discharge himself. To his surprise the front door of the hospital is a mere few steps away.

Once outside he looks back at the door, hoping for a clue as to his whereabouts. There is no sign on, above or to either side of the entrance and he finds himself standing on an ordinary street. It is as if the hospital is trying to deny that it is one, he decides. For a moment he thinks it must be a private medical facility - then concerns about the hospital bill float into his mind. He shakes them off. Whatever the cost, it feels worth it. He doesn't know exactly what medical care he's received, but he's never felt better.

The street is surprisingly empty for near mid-day, so he decides to try and find a sign that will tell him where the railway station is. He's sure he recognises one or two buildings and, gradually, more and more things become familiar. This isn't his home town, but he suddenly remembers his brother's house is just across town. Even if his brother isn't there, he can wait for him.

His mind made up, he heads in the right direction, deciding to stop for some food on the way. He digs in his pocket but comes up empty - no money and no wallet. His brother is his only hope, in that case, he decides. He'll just have to go hungry until then.

He stops at a junction, waiting for the lights to change. The cars and other vehicles that crawl past the lights are a mixture of old and obsolete vehicles. Their drivers all seem in a state of torpor. Not bothering to wonder why, he looks down at his shoes, waiting for the lights to change.

There, at his feet, two brightly coloured pieces of paper seem too enticing to ignore. He bends and, at the instant he plucks one from the floor, he stops. His name. The piece of paper has his name on it. His old name. And a time. And a place. And the promise of some sort of performance. But that's impossible.

'For One Night Only'. He exhales suddenly, a half-snort of disbelief. This is impossible. He is no longer a performer and, even if he still had been, how could this have been arranged without his knowledge? He knows the address printed on the ticket but is certain there is no theatre there. At least, there hadn't been the last time he ...

This is a mistake. Or a joke. Some sort of hoax, maybe. He can't imagine who would want to do this - he is loved, respected - but he intends to find out.

The only people he sees on his way there all seem to be ill or old, their faces grey and lined, most of them stooping or turning their gaze away. Every shop is dark; either closed, and looking like it will never open again, or boarded up. It seems like the town and its inhabitants are slowly dying.

He tries to shake off the feeling, doing his best to convince himself that it is simply a type of 'hangover' from the treatment he's received. That maybe the residue of some drug still in his system is causing him to suffer from some sort of mild depression. But he can't ignore the evidence of his eyes. Or his nose.

Put on the Mask

The fallen leaves that clog up all the gutters are the colour of rotting meat. The suggestion is so strong that he sometimes imagines he can smell the awful throat-clutching stench.

Further down the street he notices a brightly-lit building. Convinced it was in darkness only minutes earlier, he makes his way towards it. The neon is bright but not gaudy, and he recognises the name from the tickets he picked up - Théâtre du Monde de L'Ombre.

There in the display case beside the door is a poster with his name on it. The stage name he hasn't used in years. 'For One Night Only' is emblazoned across the poster. "They'll be lucky," he thinks. He'll confront the manager, demand an answer.

From the name and the design of the facade he thinks that perhaps it's a burlesque theatre. Behind the polished wood and chrome door he imagines a delicious den of modern demimondaines, tattooed and tempting. While he has no intention of treading the boards himself, he smiles at the thought of seeing a pleasing performance or two. He'll demand free tickets as some small compensation for the impertinence of the poster, of course.

The doors swing shut behind him with a satisfying thud. The lobby has wine-coloured carpets and cream walls and, like the hospital reception area, it is deserted. Another clock stares down at him from above the ticket office window. He watches its hands for a few moments before tapping the window and shouting "Hello?" Nobody comes.

He paces back and forth, wondering what to do next. Out of the corner of his eye, he catches a glimpse of someone looking at him from around a corner. He turns in time to see a head bob back out of view.

A memory rises like a startled bird. He is sure he recognises the girl. That platinum hair. Surely it's her.

He runs to the corner where she's been. Double doors stare

back at him. Above them is written the word 'Stalls'. Fearing a sudden shock, he reaches out and pushes the door open gently. Gloom stares back at him from a quiet corridor. Its floor has a gentle upward gradient.

He puts one foot through the door, despite his nervousness. An unexpected reserve of courage pulls the rest of his body through after it. "Hello?" he calls, softly. The door swings shut behind him, shutting out most of the light from the lobby.

The end of the corridor holds a velvet darkness that drinks in his gaze and gives him nothing in return. He puts out his hand to touch the comforting solidity of the wall, then makes his way slowly into the gloom.

He stops for a second. Was that someone moving in the darkness? He couldn't be sure if it was just his eyes playing tricks as they adjusted to the dark. Or was there really someone there? He feels something brush against him and he gasps, surprised. A hand grabs his lower arm.

"Is that you? Hehe ..." It must be the girl with the platinum hair. Then more hands grasp him, pulling at his arms, tugging his clothes. He tries to pull away.

"What ...? Who are you?" He begins to feel panic. It is answered by a volley of whispers, a dozen voices emerging out of the darkness, luring him on. "This way. This way. This way. This way."

Something about the way the air moves past him convinces him that the corridor has disappeared. He is somewhere else now.

As a tiny hand touches the top of his head, he jerks it sharply to one side. Trying harder to pull away now, he cannot move; the darkness already has him in its grip.

*

He'd met her first in a cafe. She was with friends; he was not. At first his broken-backed, limping words seemed to have no effect on her. Then she looked again and seemed to recognise something in him that she desired.

Her friends, all nearly identical with their dyed platinum hair and heavily painted eyes, seemed to melt away at some point during the evening until they were alone. Together.

Whenever she ordered food it was like eavesdropping on someone's prayers, murmured in pain. She toyed nervously with the thick gold bangles around her wrists. They talked about nothing, really. Inconsequential. Idiotic.

Then. "Come back with me," she'd said in her child's voice. She seemed so young. But so ready for his love. She seemed to be just what he wanted. What he needed.

Frightened of his pleasures, he was too drunk with them to stop himself. "No names," she insisted, pulling him towards her.

*

The rain entered her room, soaking them through as they lay together and kissed. "Wear the mask for me," she said. "F-for you?" Placing it over his face, she replies "Yes. It's your body I want - I don't want to have to look at your filthy feelings." It was clear to him now that he was merely a toy of flesh to her. A reverse of fortunes indeed. "Put on the mask now, Phantom. Step onto the stage and prepare for a song you will never sing; lie on my bed and prepare for the ecstasy that will never arrive."

*

A threnody of broken gasps and cries reaches his ear, a hit single of commingled despair and shock. There is nothing but darkness around him. Sounds reach him through the thick velvet nothingness.

The voices are all small. Some are angry; others simply broken, damned. Locked in. No escape from his hands.

Some of the voices are his own. "You're so much prettier than your mother." "Don't be afraid." "It's a secret, OK? Just you and me. No-one else."

A shuddering chorus of angry denials, screams, shouts shakes him like a train rumbling by, right over the grave of his still-living corpse.

He remembers crows cawing on the heath as he walked to school when he was a child. No matter how fast he walked, he could never outdistance them. He felt that same way now. They will always be there.

The voices crowd in on him now. They threaten to suffocate him, drown him out forever. They crush his mind and he screams.

*

The eye holes have grown bigger. There is a tear at one corner of the mouth. The mask is not what it was. And what if one day it should come to pieces in your hands, as you struggle to put it on? People would see your true face.

*

He awakes in the theatre. In an aisle seat. The dust and dryness of the old place fill his mouth and nose. There is someone at his side. Startled, he gasps, and turns his head. She is standing, leaning forward. "You fell asleep," she says, reaching out her hand to him. "Come on, you're due on stage."

"O-on stage? Me ... ?" He allows himself to be helped to

his feet and towards the waiting spotlight. As they move forward, the empty auditorium around them seems to fill up. The same shadowy faces, the same whispering as in his dream. The same barely suppressed anger and pain.

She tugs at his hand. Nods. Smiles. "Yes. Come on. They're all expecting you."

He allows himself to be dragged forward. "But where did you ...?" he begins to ask. His words don't seem to matter as they head towards the steps leading up to the stage. He has to prepare for his impromptu performance, trying to remember all the little tricks that made him so popular back then.

He almost trips as she pulls him up the short flight of steps. "Slow down, please."

Once on stage everything seems very different. The flats are punctured and razored in long tears, rattling in the merest breeze. Antique, dessicated vermin crunch beneath the soles of anyone unwise enough to venture onto this ghost-crowded stage. Secret pacts made in the dark are briefly revived, reverberating around and beneath the seats, echoing down the bricked-up corridors of misplaced lust.

He feels uneasy. Outside the theatre looked brand new, nothing like this near-derelict husk. "I-I just want to see the manager. You see, nobody's booked me. I've just come out of hospital this morning. Nobody's said ..."

She holds up a hand, smiles reassuringly. "Don't worry. The owner will be along very soon. Then it will all become clear."

He stands awkwardly, like a schoolboy who has been waiting outside the headmaster's office for most of his life. He becomes so used to the silence that when she speaks it is like a gunshot.

"Did you hear them? Did you dream of them? Even your own daughter. You bastard!"

He turns to look at her, startled. "What? What did you

say?"

With a few strides she is at his side. "You heard me, you filthy old bastard." There is a darkness in her eyes that scares him. How could she possibly know anything about his ... tastes? They'd spent just one night together.

When in doubt plead for mercy, that's what his mother taught him. Not that it had done her any good once his father had emptied the bottle. But he can't think of any other way out right now.

"Look. I don't know what you're talking about. Please - I'm just not up to this right now. I've only just got out of the hospital." His words seem to elicit no pity from her, so he adds, slowly: "I had an accident. I was lucky to survive." At that, a slow cruel smile creeps along her lips. The smile seems to plant an image in his mind.

The accident. Is it an accident when someone pushes you, trying to silence your tongue, your words smashing apart on a hard concrete floor at the end of a long fall down a stairwell? An accident. That was what he'd called it, but now ...

She stands before him, shaking her head. "No accident. I was sent to fetch you." A flicker of understanding passes through his mind, but before he can grasp its meaning, she grasps his chin and forces him to look at her.

Then the girl with platinum hair removes her mask and he sees the truth at last. Hope falls, reeling headlong into a deep pit. He hasn't seen her since they took her away. He hasn't been allowed to.

"You! B - but we ... ," he begins. "Not for the first time!" she hisses, anger nearly strangling her words at birth.

He draws in his breath sharply. "But how are you here? You're still alive."

She slides the wide gold bangles from her wrists and holds them out to him. They bear the ugly deep scars of fatal wounds. They hadn't told him - he hadn't even been allowed

Put on the Mask

that.

"D-dead," he breathes, in a voice as hollow as his every promise.

*

"I don't want to see your disgusting fucking face! Put on the mask, he's coming; the ultimate audience, the final critic."

*

He looks up and the small theatre is suddenly full. There must be hundreds of them. None of their faces are clear. There is a light in his eyes but he can still make out that they are all children. Every seat is filled by a small figure, just like the children's matinees he used to perform at. Some are smaller than others but they are all silent. All gazing at him.

He looks behind him. She is standing there like some wardress, ready to punish any infraction of the unguessed-at rules. He realises that he is dressed in his old stage clothes, now spotted with mould and hanging in tattters.

A bang at the back of the theatre makes him peer into the darkness. A door has just slammed. The figure who has entered strides forward purposefully. As he passes each row of seats, the figures of the phantom children evaporate into nothing, leaving not even a wisp behind.

Now the man has reached the front row. His appearance causes the ragged figure on stage to gasp and back away in fright, only to be intercepted by the girl and forced back to his former place.

To some the man would seem smartly dressed, to others it would appear overdone. Gloved and hatted. His movements are slightly too precise, as if considered by an actor, calculated for maximum effect. But the face itself is hardly finished. The gloved hands appear imprecise and clumsy.

The shabby figure on the stage does not dare turn around again but does not want to look at his 'audience' either. He stares into the painful glare of the spotlight, praying for blindness. He can feel her hate-filled gaze upon him. "The stage is yours, old man. This is your time. Give us one of your standards. Sing 'Light As a Feather'," she instructs.

She looks at the solitary seated figure. "For your pleasure, sir," she says, indicating the pathetic figure in rags stood before her. The man nods enthusiastically. With a wave from him, the tiny orchestra pit suddenly becomes peopled by musicians.

Every member of the small orchestra looks emaciated and terrified. Their sharp elbows poke through the faded cloth of their striped clothing. The leader, hollow-eyed, looks up at the figure on stage for a moment before turning to his companions. Bows begin to scrape dryly, the horns emit a few spare, wheezy notes.

It is a tune he is familiar with, he thinks, though it is hard to make it out at first, given this near funereal rendition.

The sudden impact of her shoe in his back reminds him he is expected to perform. Afraid to begin, yet more afraid of what might happen if he doesn't, he begins to croak out the first line of his most famous song. His voice catches, and he stands shamefaced while his body shakes with a coughing spasm.

The solitary punter looks up. In a voice rough and rusty he asks, "What's this? Has the actor forgotten his lines ... the singer, his song? No!"

More afraid than ever of the consequences of failure, the tattered performer begins again. The orchestra begins scraping away once more. His dry old vocal cords begin to grind out the words.

"When we're - togethe-e-er, I (cough) feel as light as - a -

feathe-e-er, My heart is - " The words stop as his chest fills with pain, his throat with the dust of desolation and disappointment. Falling to his knees, he struggles to keep his spine straight for a few seconds, then falls flat on his face, choking.

She steps forward, looking down at him with glee as he jerks with pain, his eyes rolling back. When he is finally still, she clasps her hands together in front of her. She kicks the limp body just once. The impact dislodges the mask he has worn all his life, revealing the ugliness and corruption it has covered for too long.

From the front row, the call of "Encore! Encore!" is spat through brown, sharpened teeth. The solitary audience member's gunshot-loud clapping sends clouds of dust up into the air, drifting slowly towards the stage to rain down upon the collapsed figure lying there.

The punter stands, picking up the expensive-looking coat laid across the seat beside him, and turns to leave. He glances once over his shoulder at the heap upon the stage, the man's daughter standing over him, trembling, hands clasped in prayer to some imaginary god of revenge and redemption. Both victims. He grins in malicious satisfaction, enjoying the symmetry. As he walks towards the exit, he yells over his shoulder: "Your finest moment!"

The heavy door swings shut with a final thud as he leaves the theatre. He spares a single glance at the poster beside the door. Across it a cheaply printed two-colour red-and-white banner reads 'Tonight - and every night!'

The street down which he walks has changed beyond all recognition, as if a theatre flat had fallen to reveal the truth hidden behind it. Along its length a million other theatre fronts show a million identical banners.

Against The Grain

Atwill's back is barely visible through the raging dance of particles. It doesn't help that the lenses of my goggles are so scratched that I have to turn my head slightly to the right in order to see anything at all.

Despite the rope connecting us, he seems distant and often lost in this perpetual sandstorm. The lifeline allows us to be no more than three-and-a-half feet from each other, but I feel trapped and alone for much of the time, trudging endlessly on. Communication is normally impossible; the batteries to our intercoms died many months ago, so now we are reduced to hand signals or, when greater urgency is needed, shouting with our foreheads pressed against each other.

Even then, the wind whips away our words, the sand scrubbing them smooth of any meaning.

It's so difficult to remember exactly how long ago we set off, though I know there were three of us when we began. And we left several others behind us, awaiting our return and their rescue.

My recollection of our arrival is hazy, though I do remember that our pilot was killed in the crash. My wife is waiting for me back there somewhere. She and the others are counting on us. It was decided that the three strongest, of whom I was one, should set off to seek help. That was so long ago.

We equipped ourselves from the possessions that had survived the forced landing and set off, not knowing how long we would be gone but, given the terrible conditions we faced, praying it would be just days. Then we wandered out into the wilderness of wind and sand, striking the wall within only a few hours.

Its alternately pitted and smooth surfaces formed

themselves out of the swirling grains, bronze and grey in colour, and at first we thought we'd found the perimeter of some settlement. Only after walking along its length for several hours did we come to believe that it went on forever and that there was nobody, or nothing, alive behind it.

*

"It's a boat," yelled Atwill as he pressed his mouth to my ear. I, in turn, pressed my mouth against his headgear: "A boat? Here?" He simply turned again and nodded. I knew that Atwill hoped to find some answers inside it.

As far as we knew there was no water here at all, let alone enough to make a boat necessary. But from where we stood, pressed against it, it did look like a boat of some sort, that the current had caught and later abandoned haphazardly.

It's keel was turned towards us, towering over us but affording us some protection form the wind at least. It seemed utterly black yet a lighter colour was beginning to show through where the sand had worn away at it.

Atwill motioned and I nodded back. We began to move around the 'boat' to see what lay on the other side. The wind caught us fiercely as we rounded the end of the huge object but we clung together and finally found ourselves in a position to clamber onto the shape.

We spent some minutes clambering over it, acquainting ourselves with shapes that, even at this skewed angle, looked like they could be cabins or deck lockers. There was even something resembling a binnacle. But we couldn't find an opening anywhere and everything was the same universal black colour. There didn't even seem to be any portholes or windows either and it seemed to me to be made of some sort of smooth stone rather than the expected metal or wood.

After 10 minutes or so, disappointment took over and we

gestured to each other that we should abandon the supposed vessel. We slipped over the side like ocean weary travellers leaving their sinking ship.

As we trudged disconsolately on, I wondered what the object could really be. The insane thought even occurred to me that it may be a sculpture of a ship, never intended for use or practically but merely to imitate a sort of life.

I looked back once and saw the shape appear and reappear as the sand whipped around it. I wondered how many years it would take before the sand wore it away altogether or just buried it and forgot it.

*

Food and water was thankfully never a problem as, along the enormous and seemingly unending wall, there were doorways, held closed against the perpetual scouring wind with simple locks. Inside each of these identical rooms were four beds, a rudimentary bathroom and a locker filled with bland but edible food. Priest, our companion, expressed his doubts about the food, fearing it was drugged. But, as Atwill said after our own supplies had run out, we had no other choice except starvation.

But we haven't seen one of these 'way stations' for two days now and I feel light-headed and weak. Though he is bigger than me, Atwill must be feeling it too.

My body aches more than normal and I feel as though I should simply lie face down in the sand and let it swallow me alive. If I had another way to die I might choose that instead. But I don't.

Within days of setting off it became clear that we were making our way through an excessive and labyrinthine architecture of stone and metal; a maze whose origin and purpose was unknown. Atwill asserted several times that the floor upon which we were walking had a slight incline and that, according to his compass, the structure was slowly winding in upon itself. He answered with a disdainful look when I asked if he could be sure if his compass would work properly in the conditions in which we found ourselves.

Visibility was so poor that all we could do was cling to the enormous wall that appeared before us on the first morning. The top wasn't visible in the howling flurry of the sand but we estimated it must be hundreds of feet high. As Atwill had said, the wall seemed to twist and curve in unexpected ways, always leading us in another direction, away to our left.

That, together with the constant whorls of sand that appeared before us and the absurdly fast changes in wind direction, meant that we never knew in what direction we were truly heading. The sand seemed to set us a new challenge every few minutes, rebuilding itself relentlessly before dissolving away in an instant to be replaced equally as quickly by a new puzzle.

Whatever we do the wind tugs at us or pushes us, pulls us back or shoves us sideways. And despite it all, we spend each day drenched in sweat from our exertions. To suggest that we rest for even just a day would be like admitting defeat; we might just as well put a gun to our heads.

The dreadful ache in my hips, back and legs begs me to stop but we daren't halt before what passes for nightfall here, when the light changes from a torn orange to a darker shade that belongs to no hour of the day that I recognise. I feel as though I've stopped being a man and have become simply a machine for walking.

Always there is the agonising song of the wind, whistling or grumbling, as it hurls the sand hard against the edges of the buildings. Wherever you go it is there, following every turn and curve on this seemingly eternal journey. It has always got there before you and maybe it has even helped to create this place, bleakly hammering it into the curious shapes and whorls that adorn some of the low buildings huddled against the huge wall.

At first I plugged myself into my personal music player, drowning out the constant sound. But when the songs began to seem as monotonous as the roar and sigh outside, I abandoned the player in one of our nightly shelters.

Once, several weeks after we started walking and several months ago now, the storms stopped. That can't be true, of course, but it seemed as though they stopped. We found ourselves in a silent, still pocket hidden within the storms. The air cleared of particles for a minute, only a minute, and we could see across the floor of shallow, undulating dunes. There was a far wall; huge and distant, disappearing into a rumour of sky. Only then was it perfectly clear to us that we were inside some enormous structure and not merely crawling along its surface.

Within seconds of us removing our goggles and protective masks, the sand had lashed at us again, stinging our faces and forcing us to huddle into ourselves. But we had seen something that had both made our hearts sink and given us hope.

*

I remember the day when we lost Priest. He was last in line and for some reason he cut the rope and ran off into the shifting beige nothingness. I noticed the slackening in the tension of the lifeline and signalled Atwill. Somehow we came across his body later that day, even though the direction seemed impossible.

He'd been driven mad by the constant storm and had stripped himself of his headgear and clothing. The sand had flayed the skin from him and was eating into his flesh moment by moment, exposing the white of his bones. We dragged what was left of him over to the wall, heaped sand over him and left him there.

*

A day later we came across something that could have been a machine or an animal, still only partially buried. We had examined the jagged thick remains for some time but it had eluded any definitive explanation.

That evening, at one of the waystations that allowed us food and shelter, Atwill insisted it was some sort of flyer. That it was proof there were inhabitants here after all and that we only had to find them.

I pointed out that the white spars could easily have been bones, scoured of all flesh by long months or even years of the persistent grit and wind, and that the inhabitants may just be giant flying beasts somehow adapted to live in these harsh conditions.

Atwill was clearly unhappy with my conjecture. "You know, Zucco, I don't know why I bother asking your opinion on anything. You always find the most depressing 'explanation' for everything," he'd snarled.

I pointed out that this was probably because I was a scientist and, therefore, a stranger to the inherent dangers of incautious optimism. Or wishful thinking.

*

The wall is gargantuan and seems to be made up of many different metals and types of stone. Several times we have been obliged to cling to it, covering ourselves in a tarpaulin or just huddling even further into our sand-caked clothes, trying to escape the wind as it attempts to tear us free and send us who knows where as it flings us into the grim-coloured sky (if sky it is).

Once, just after the worst of the renewed storm had passed, I found a collection of small objects pushed into a fissure where two sorts of metal were joined together. They were small intricately-designed things. Not exactly round but not really bearing a strong relation to any other shape either.

I tucked my jacket over my head and looked at them in as much detail as I could there and then. There were a mystery to me.

At our way station stop that night, I showed the others (as Priest was still with us then). They turned them over and over in their fingers, offering various explanations as to what they might be. They were obviously made rather than hewn by nature and had various indentations and markings on their small surfaces.

Might they be toys, said Atwill, hidden by a desperate child? Or maybe some form of mysterious communication devices, conjectured Priest. I wondered where there were so many of them ... nearly a dozen in number ... and if they somehow fitted together to form a 'book' of some sort, a chronicle of disaster or progress, a warning or a map?

They lay on the floor between us, giving nothing away and serving only to puzzle and infuriate.

Priest smiled, his parched lips cracking as he did so. "Well at least it proves one thing. We're not the first ones to come this way." He saw that as a sign of hope, of escape; I simply feared that we would find the bodies of those who had secreted these objects away in the days ahead ... if their remains hadn't been completely hidden by the sands.

*

The sky is a different colour this morning; a greyness has

crept into it, although its brightness hasn't dimmed at all. The wall has veered off in yet another direction and we are spiralling still further to our left.

We are both quite weak now and every step takes three times as much effort as it did a few days ago. I doubt either of us will last much longer. I am long past hoping that we will find anything here except wind and sand; it seems to be the whole world.

There is a steady incline to the floor here and Atwill seems to be slowing his progress even more than me. He is now only over a foot in front of me. Several times I have deliberately dropped back. I don't want him to turn and see me that close, to realise that he is weakening so badly.

The wind has changed direction now, growing even faster and tugging at our clothes, pulling them upwards for the first time. It's as if the wind is leaving. Maybe its journey is done.

The sand inclines steeply. It's the first time we've ever seen that, too. We begin to climb. After several minutes, I feel the tension on the line slacken and then nearly stumble over Atwill, who has sunk down in front of me. I do the same, my knees crunching painfully into the hard sand.

I look at him, his head sunk between his shoulders, and realise that he has both hands outstretched, palms flat against a wall. I look around, peering hard through the departing storm. We are surrounded on three sides by walls. Impossible!

The opposite wall is now only a mere dozen yards away whereas when we'd seen it the previous time it had seemed a mile or more away.

I shake Atwill, trying to get some sort of response. I yell in his ear but he doesn't answer. Then I see where his hands are resting, his fingers partially covering some letters stencilled onto the surface.

I pull his hand away and feel a blackness creep into me as I see the full extent of the thing covering the wall. Brushing at it, the sand falls away to reveal a sprawling diagram of some sort. Among the squares and crossroads, squashed between the temples and dead industrial zones, I can see the shape of our fate. The city seems to be gargantuan, going on forever, lost in distance as the shapes of its avenues and cul-de-sacs crawl up the wall.

There, trapped in the centre of the sprawling map is a large circular pattern. And there, at the dead centre of the winding maze, are the words that Atwill's fingers had covered - "You are here."

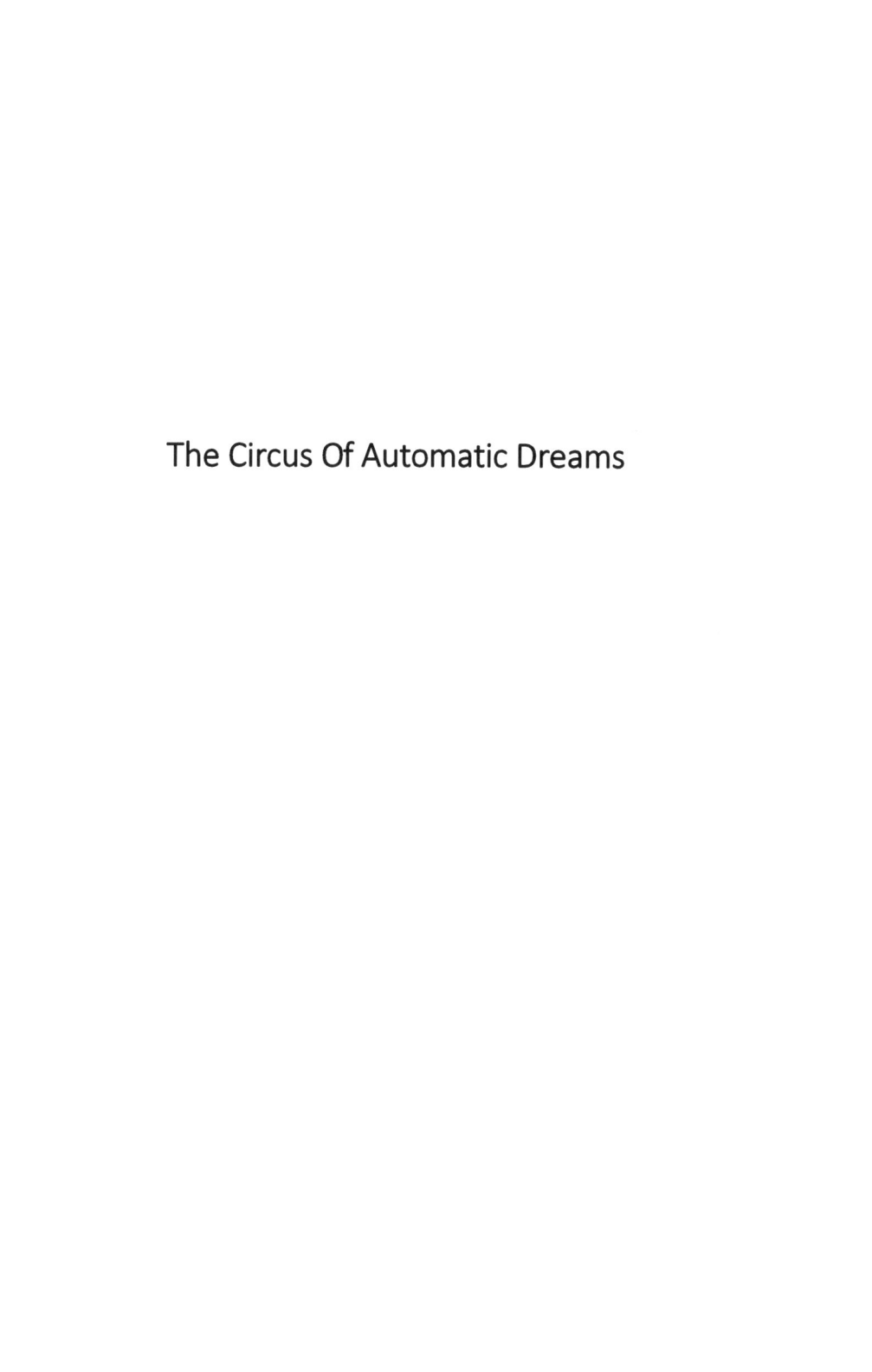

The Circus Of Automatic Dreams

Vertically speaking, Sam was very much a horizontal man these days. For the last three years he'd rarely bothered to get out of bed. Except on those dreaded occasions when the circus came to town.

There was no big top, no barking ringmaster with a large whip, no dazzlingly-dressed women or impressively well-trained animals - nothing to draw the attention, in fact. In fact (and facts were what Sam usually liked to rely on) it wasn't a circus at all.

But Sam always knew when it was due to arrive. He could feel it coming from days and miles away.

*

A millennium passed in just two weeks, seemingly, as Sam's dreams grew deeper and darker, his waking hours ever shorter. Until finally sleep claimed him completely and he 'woke' into a dream from which he knew there was no release.

He found himself in a small boat. It drifted sluggishly on a narrow canal sandwiched between tall, dark buildings, many of which had begun to crumble into the water. Sam looked at the single paddle in his hand, then up at the narrow chink of greyish-blue sky above him. He somehow remembered this place, though he didn't know where from.

Finally, just before a grey brick bridge connecting two monolithic factory buildings, he came across a small stretch of pathway. Sam steered towards it and stepped ashore gingerly. Moments later, the boat gave a revolting gurgling sound and sank beneath the canal's opaque waters. A few silver bubbles were all that remained of it.

The suspicion sneaked into Sam's mind that the boat had actually been an amphibious animal.

He sighed heavily, then looked up the only street that led from the pathway. It was narrow and dirty, and on the nearest corner stood a pub.

The structure looked dangerously dilapidated but there was nowhere else for him to go; none of the other buildings in the street even had doors. As he approached, he could see a faint light coming from behind the filthy windows. He stopped and looked up at the sign on the front of the building. Although several letters were missing their outline could still clearly be seen, haloed by grime. 'The Morpheus Arms'. What else would it be called? thought Sam.

He walked through the door, which hung unevenly from the top hinge. His footsteps crunched on the debris of broken brick and shattered glass. Though the place was in ruins, a cheery barman stood behind the well-lit bar, ready to dispense liquid cheer to whoever came in. "What can I get you, sir?" he almost chirped.

Sam noticed that the man's words were muffled. When he stepped closer he saw that there was a thick sheet of glass at the front of the bar. Peering through the glass, he couldn't be sure whether the man had been caged in alive or whether he was some sort of automaton. Whichever it was, he seemed happy enough with his lot, and Sam bemoaned the fact he couldn't actually have a drink. God knows I need one, he thought, glancing enviously at the bright bottles behind the bar.

A soft cough came from behind Sam. He turned and there, in the corner of the ruined bar room, sat the undeclared ringmaster of this psychic circus. "So you found us. But, of course, you did ... ," said the man. He was dressed in an old-fashioned dress jacket with a purple silk shirt under it. The shirt had several noticeable tears and it was open at the neck.

As on at least one past occasion, the man wore the face of a friend of Sam's grandfather, with a thin moustache and slightly crooked nose.

Sam crunched his way over to the table where the man sat. He regretted the fact that he was without a drink even more now that he was able to look into the man's broken lizard eyes. Sam felt that sarcasm was one of the few weapons in his meagre arsenal. "So tell me, oh great and powerful Oz, what have you got in store for me this time?"

The man motioned to the seat opposite him. "Sit down," he said, then took an obscenely large gulp of whisky. Sam shook his head.

"Why am I here again?" asked Sam. The man looked down at the table, tracing a wet glass mark with his finger. He repeated the word 'again', seeming genuinely puzzled. Sam admired his acting skills if nothing else.

Sam raised his voice. "Well, why am I here?"

"WELL ...," yelled the man, in clear mockery of Sam. He leaned forward and leered. "Do you remember that little girl in school, during the third ... ," he began.

Sam leapt in, cutting him off. "I've paid for that already. I pay for it every day."

The man chuckled maliciously. "Oh yes, that's water under the bridge, isn't it, Sam? And that bridge has been burnt, hasn't it? Well and truly ..."

"Then why do you keep doing this to me? Is it some sort of punishment?"

The man twisted his face up in mock contemplation for a moment. "Mmmm, yes. Call it that, if you like."

"But what am I being punished for?" asked Sam.

"Because you don't brush your teeth often enough. Because you don't like the colour blue. Because you don't call your sister every week. Are those good enough reasons for you? There are probably plenty of other things that you don't do either. Everyone has done and left undone plenty of things they deserve to be punished for ... plenty." When he'd finished speaking the man's face became a mask of malice.

"You're just a good old-fashioned sadist, aren't you?" he man chuckled. "Got it in one. Now get lost."

I'm not going to follow orders, thought Sam. I'll just sit down here, opposite him and wait until he gets tired and releases me. The man stared at him for a few seconds, as if divining Sam's thoughts, then chuckled softly to himself.

Then Sam felt his feet moving, even though that was the last thing he wanted. The barman in his fish tank watched as Sam passed slowly in front of him.

Within a minute Sam found himself outside once more, staring down into the oily, thick water of the canal. A dead animal bobbed to the surface, offering up its corpse smile in mockery. 'You're just as helpless as I am,' it said in Sam's head as it drifted away on its back, stiff paws pointed skyward.

As he stared at the rictus grin, Sam remembered (though he was prepared to admit it may have been a false memory) once when he was nine years of age, he'd got lost when returning from playing with his cousin. He'd wandered onto a patch of waste ground covered with enormous plants. Hidden among them was a burned-out car.

It was late afternoon and there was just enough of the back seat left to provide a comfortable perch. So Sam climbed in through the open back door and had a nap.

When he woke it was getting dark and, as he clambered out over the remains of the driver's seat, his foot caught something in the foot well. He strained his eyes to see what it was in the gloom, before hurtling off in a breathless run for home, convinced he'd been staring into the fixed smile and dark dead sockets of a charred skull.

"Probably just a dog," Sam had muttered to himself,

wanting to be convinced.

Sam looked around him. Everything was dusty and desolate. On the windowsill of the pub, under its broken lead-glassed window, sat a rusted dart without any flights. He picked it up, noticing its end was blunt, and stuffed it into his pocket. This time he intended to have evidence of his stay - a brief one, he hoped - in this town that lay at the back of the wardrobe, in the back of beyond or the back of his brain.

He walked up the street, the pavement crunching grittily under his feet. Both sides were taken up with the backs of anonymous industrial buildings, featureless and depressing. At the end of the street he found a main street.

It stretched away in both directions and there was a side road opposite where he stood. Sam took in the scene slowly. There wasn't a single person in sight. No cars drove by. Every single shop was closed down, either shuttered up or missing windows and doors altogether.

"It's like the end of the world," he said loudly, hoping to evoke some response from somewhere, anywhere. None came.

He picked a direction and began walking. He might as well try and walk out of this desolate hangover of a place. But after just five minutes, Sam began to feel tired. Really tired. A strange kind of lethargy crept into his body, seemingly from outside. He wondered if there was a colourless, odourless gas washing over the area. If so, he would be its only victim. That seemed like a waste to him. He giggled at the absurdity of the thought.

Sam staggered over to the doorway of a former bed shop. Bed. That's a really good idea, he thought, and slouched heavily through the gap where the window used to be. He looked around blearily. There were no beds anywhere to be seen. 'They must have had a sale' said his brain.

He limped and foot-dragged through to the back of the

shop. The area had obviously been a large showroom at one time. A large skylight let a generous slice of daylight into the space. The light somehow made Sam even more tired. He carefully let himself down on to the floor, which he was surprised to find was quite clean.

Sam lay on his back, closed his eyes, and concentrated on breathing as slowly as he could. From the ceiling, flower petals began to spiral down like tiny Da Vinci devices, covering his face and chest. Grateful for the respite, he lay there, savouring the light pressure and lingering perfume as they fluttered onto his eyelids, lips and cheeks.

In his state of lethargy, Sam didn't realise there was danger until he found it hard to breathe. The weight on his chest and arms grew every second, and the breath was being crushed out of him. He struggled to move below what felt like a ton of petals as they clogged his nostrils and covered his lips. He tried to spit but this simply made more petals stick to him. He struggled to rise, pushed back down hard in his floral prison.

The he detected movement in the petals around his face and a voice reached him faintly through his stopped-up ears. "Let me help," it said and he felt soft fingers on his cheek. As the petals were cleared away from his eyelids, he could open his eyes at last. Above him he saw a girl's face. She smiled and reached out her hands to help him up.

Sam stood and brushed the last of the petals from his pollen-flecked clothes, stuffing them into his pocket. He took a good look at the girl. She was dressed oddly in peach and cherry coloured clothing and could be a circus performer, he supposed. Still he was grateful to her and only slightly worried by the blood he noticed under her fingernails; it could simply be from the crushed petals, he reasoned.

Beneath her disreputable eyes and aquiline nose sat a barnstorming mouth. "Hello," she said.

"Uuum ... hello. Who are you? I haven't seen anyone else

about ..."

The girl shook her head. "No, it's a Bank Holiday today, isn't it?" as if the comment explained the devastated streets outside. "I'm Pollay. I live here. What are you doing here?"

Sam rubbed his hand through his hair. "I felt sleepy, so I came in here to sleep. Does that happen often?" He looked over his shoulder at the pile of petals, which were slowly dissolving in a pool of sunlight.

"Only when you're around," she giggled.

"Well, thank you. I couldn't breathe. You may have saved my life."

Pollay looked him up and down. "I think I did, you know."

Sam liked her but something warned him against flirting with her. "I need to be getting on. I feel wide awake now. Which is the quickest way out of town?"

Pollay seemed puzzled by something he'd said. " Umm ... I don't know. I've got a map somewhere. Follow me."

"Do you live here then?"

"Yes, just behind the shop ... " she began before turning her head sharply. Impossibly, Sam was sure he saw her ears prick up. Her head jerked from side to side, obviously listening for something. "Rats!" she hissed. "They're as big as cats ..."

Before Sam could blink, Pollay had darted away into the gloom of the huge shop. There were scuffling sounds and within seconds he saw a huge furry body scurry through a pool of sunlight and into the darkness at the back of the showroom. Slightly spooked by the size of the beast, Sam involuntarily took several steps back. The girl hadn't been exaggerating. It was by far the largest rat he'd ever seen.

Pollay dashed past him, almost on all fours. "Don't worry, I'll get it," she hissed as she sped past Sam. "Help yourself," he replied in a low voice.

There was an agonised squeal as the speeding girl

obviously caught up with the furry monstrosity. Sam clapped. "Well done," he said, starting to walk towards Pollay before the awful sounds of crunching and slurping halted his footsteps. That explains the blood under her fingernails, he thought. He turned away and walked back into the daylight, trying not to throw up.

Several seconds passed before Pollay emerged, having carefully wiped her mouth and hands. She dropped the remains of the rat on the floor to one side of Sam. "That's taken care of that," she said, matter-of-factly. "Now I'll get you that map."

Sam just wanted to get out of there but he knew he'd be wandering aimlessly without some more concrete knowledge of where he needed to go. He needed that map. "O - OK," he said.

He turned to follow her and then realised he'd have to pass the rat's carcass. He took a deep breath and made to follow Pollay. As he passed the dead thing on which she had been feasting, he noticed it had the face of a human child. He tried to suppress his gasp.

"It's just through here," said Pollay. Sam turned to look and saw her open a metal door covered in flaking green paint. Beyond it, in the dark, a figure moved slowly. As it moved, the darkness moved with it, threatening to break out into the daylight, polluting it for good. It was something he remembered from a nightmare long ago. It had clung to him all these years and it made him break out into a sweat, made his legs work under him. They took him out into the street and down the middle of the road, dodging debris and a pile of broken furniture.

Behind him he could hear Pollay shouting after him. At first it was simply pleas for him to return, then it turned to threats. By the time her voice had become that of someone else, much deeper and darker, he was mercifully almost out of earshot.

Sam didn't stop running until the shattered street dropped away on either side of him, becoming tattered rags and broken wood like a long-abandoned theatre set. Soon there was nothing left of it at all and he found himself in open countryside as twilight began to fall.

To his left was a snow-covered road forking off, with a vicious cross-wind whipping across it. To his right lay a field full of burning dancers, screaming in their pirouetting pyrotechnics yet never putting a foot wrong and all, Sam knew, against their will.

The only option was to keep going straight ahead, into the wall of darkness that held God knows what. "This is the worst dream I've never had," he muttered, tempted to slow his pace but knowing at the same time that it wouldn't help things one bit. In his gut he knew that if he didn't go to the darkness, it would come to him.

Dreading what lay ahead, Sam forced himself to plod onwards, closing his eyes for a moment to see which was the blacker - the darkness inside him or that which lay ahead. But there was no difference as far as he could see, before he realised that they were both the same thing.

As he drew closer to the wall of darkness, a small room began forming out of the black and he moved towards it. Yes, he could see something definite now. It was clean and white and had shining things in it.

It was only when he stepped inside it and the walls closed to form a rectangle that he knew what it was. He remembered it was the shower room of a local brothel that he would visit quite close to the end of his life; desperate to feel some sort of heat before the cold claimed him for good, closing over him and obscuring him from everyone's memory.

A despairing coldness began to wash over him. He felt idiotically sorry for himself and begged the fates that he wouldn't be driven to this in his last, difficult years.

He couldn't face the fact that his last sexual encounter would be with a bored, loveless girl who probably wished he was already dead and not bothering her with his withered old body. He'd feel cheated by that.

Sam suddenly began to feel icy cold. There was frost starting to creep out of every surface. "Oh yes, well done. A lovely metaphor for the chill of old age," he muttered, sarcastically. He was beginning to despise his own subconscious.

He knew he had to get out of there before he became frozen solid. The plughole of the shower seemed like the blackest thing in the room, so he decided to seek escape through the dark. He leaned down and stuck his fingers into the opening, pulling as hard as he could. At first he thought he was wasting his time, but eventually the black hole began to loosen and he was able to widen it enough to slip inside.

"Here we go," he thought as he plunged feet first into the blackness. He didn't know where he would end up but it was better than where he was. He slid and slipped down a pitch-black slide. When he came to a halt, it was suddenly and with a bump. Everything was still black. He felt around him and found himself sitting on short, tough grass.

He sat and peered into the nothingness. No point getting up if I can't see where I am, he thought.

Gradually, out of the blackness, parts of a town began to appear, as if someone was holding down the 'fast forward' button on the dawn. Red brick houses took asymmetrical twists along a hillside. Sam stood up and began walking towards the nearest street. He hadn't had very good experience with the street he'd come across previously, but he remained optimistic.

The street was steep and the climb wasn't easy. Sam knew

what he'd find at the top. He tramped past dozens of anonymous terraced houses, each differing only slightly from the one before it.

He breathed a weary sigh of recognition when he reached the top. He stood at the junction of five streets, all heading downwards steeply. And there, at the corner where two terraces disappeared downwards, was a shop.

Sam had never seen it before, not even in a photograph, but he knew what it would look like and where he would find it. The shop's frontage was narrow, crammed onto the tiny corner. There were four steps leading up to the door, with two narrow display windows facing in towards the steps.

He walked up to the steps and stood at the bottom. Each of the display windows was empty and the shop looked as if it had closed down, with green paint peeling from the woodwork. Yet behind the glass pane in the door, cluttered with advertising stickers for lollipops long unavailable and pleas to help find missing cats, there was a light. And a small, discreet sign hanging on a piece of tatty string read 'Open'.

Before he walked up the steps and pushed open the door, Sam already knew who and what he would find inside.

The radio was on. His Aunty Jane always had the radio on. The song was all wrong, of course. "... raindrops on leather and whispered old kittens, these are a few of my dangerous things ... " it misquoted quietly in the background.

There was a short woman wearing mainly green behind the counter, sitting on a stool. She stood and came around the counter, reaching out to hug him. "Sam, lad. It's been so long." She beamed up at him.

"It's been no time at all," said Sam, shaking his head. He extricated himself from Jane's python-like grip.

There was something wet and wrong in her breathing. The beginnings of the cancer that would eventually take her, he imagined. He hadn't noticed it when he was a boy ... but then maybe it hadn't been there. Maybe it was being supplied now for his benefit; a very un-special effect.

"How's your mum?"

Sam pondered for a second or two the best way to explain to his aunt that her sister was dead, that she was dead too, and only alive in any way because of a rather cruel dream that was being inflicted on him. The best way to explain was not to explain, he decided. It wouldn't make any difference anyway. "She's fine, thanks."

On the newspaper rack near the door of the cramped shop he noticed the headline on The Sunk newspaper. 'Elvis Still Dead Shock'. He allowed himself a soft chuckle before looking back at his aunt who was still smiling broadly. She'd never run a corner shop when she was alive, he remembered. She'd been a secretary for the police force, right up until her death.

Behind the counter of the tiny shop was a door. If he went through it, Sam knew that the living room from the old house in Jamaica Street would be there. On the mantelpiece would be the photo of Uncle David, smiling out from a day long before he was crushed to death in an accident at work. The carpet and furnishing would smell faintly of lavender. He wouldn't even think about going through the door, he decided. His aunt talked on and he tried to listen.

Sam began to leaf through the issue of 'Dracula Sucks!' comic that his aunt had handed him. He'd collected it when he was about nine and smiled at the lively illustrations, struggling to jump off the page at him. The centre pages were missing, blank. In place of the comic panels were two white pages with the words "Get out! Go and find her!" scrawled across them in scratchy charcoal letters.

He shook his head. Go and find who, he wondered. But then a sense of unease came over him and he thought that maybe he should follow the advice being offered.

"Look, I'd best go, Aunty."

"Oh no, love, not so soon. I hardly ever see you now," she complained.

Sam smiled ruefully at the thought. 'I'll pop in again soon. I promise." With that he dashed out of the door and headed for one of the precipitous streets that led down into the unfamiliar yet boringly predictable town. He glanced behind him once and the shop had turned to crumbling pumice. Maybe Aunty had decided to act out the part of Lot's wife, he thought, then picked up the pace.

Soon he had to try and slow himself down. The hill was so steep that gravity was getting the better of him. Going downhill, Sam thought. How appropriate. His mental chuckle turned to panic within seconds as he lost his footing and began to roll head over heels downhill, like a human pinball in a grimy, red brick machine.

A kaleidoscope of grey and red, punctuated just once by labrador yellow, whirled past him (or, rather, he whirled past it) as he sped towards the bottom of the hill.

He came to a tumbleover slipback bounceup stop at the bottom of the hill, ending up on the far pavement of the junction, having been narrowly missed by a small, yellow car driven by a man in full clown make-up. The driver beeped indignantly with his bulb horn as he sped away.

Sam dusted himself off and looked around. The monotony of the grimy terraced houses was broken by the wrought iron fence of a large park. He walked a few yards to the gate and read the words that made up part of the design. Victoria Park. Of course, he thought, I could be anywhere with a name like that.

He went through the gate, passed the packed flower beds and headed towards the cast iron bandstand. The fountain near the gate was switched off and, by the looks of things, hadn't worked for some years. The water in the basin was red;

strange, dark fish were visible from time to time as they came close to the surface.

Sam backed away in distaste. Only then did he notice a woman in a blue coat standing at the far side of the bandstand. She looked as if she was waiting for someone. When she turned her head to one side, his heart leapt up his throat and did its best to stop his breath.

It was her. He hadn't seen her for years - and couldn't remember where - but he knew he loved her. More than anything. He didn't know why Helen would be here, but he didn't care.

Sam tore up a handful of tulips from a flower bed, shaking off clumps of earth before twisting off the bottom of the stems to make them look more presentable.

She didn't see him as he approached. "H - H - Helen?"

She turned and looked at him with hazel eyes. "Oh, hello, Sam," she said. She didn't seem that pleased to see him. "I didn't expect to see you here. Not today."

"U-um, no. I just ... happened to be passing," he said, before he could stop himself. A voice inside his head reproached him for peddling cliches and told him to hold out the flowers, if that wasn't too much trouble. "I got these for you, Helen. I hope you like them."

Helen smiled and nodded. "Thank you," she said, brushing some spots of dirt off the petals.

Sam's dreamheart thumped in his chest. "I - I ... haven't seen you for so long." Then a nagging memory told him that they'd parted company in some manner. Things were vague but Sam felt an apology was necessary.

"Listen. I'm really sorry for what happened between us. It was all my fault. And I've changed, I promise. So I ... er, was hoping you'd think about coming back to me. Please?" Sam had no idea if he'd changed, but he hoped to pick up signals from Helen later and adjust his course to suit.

"Look at where we are," she said, extending her arm to indicate their surroundings as if pointing things out to a slow child. The colour had drained out of the flowers he'd given her, staining her hands and leaving her holding a grey bouquet. She dropped them on the floor and reached in her coat pocket for a handkerchief.

"I can't come back and I'm not sure I'd want to anyway. You killed me, Sam! Alcohol and petrol don't make a happy combination, do they?" He jumped back as if Helen had thrown boiling water in his face.

Sam turned away from her and tried to push his memories of that night under a heavy stone at the back of his mind. The party, the noise, the shattered windscreen, the tang of her blood in his mouth, the flashing blue lights; all of it was flattened as the weight of the stone crashed down on it. He stood panting, his hands on his knees, lips moving as he silently begged the memories to leave him in peace.

His mood was broken by a noise from behind him. It sounded like two elephants rushing a door. When he turned to look, he was astonished to see two huge grey wolves loping across the park towards them. Behind the creatures was a huge hole in the boundary hedge. They were heading straight for Helen. How had she not heard them?

"Behind you," yelled Sam, pointing.

"What is this, a bloody pantomime?" she demanded.

Sam waved his arms at her. "No, no - look behind you!" By now one of the large animals was just a few yards behind her. He was afraid she wouldn't get away in time and began to run towards her. But then she glanced behind her, screamed and began running across the large lawn at an alarming speed.

Sam began to run himself as the second wolf bounded towards him. The last he saw of Helen, she was climbing a tree, out of reach of the wolf despite its size. In the very last glimpse he had of her he was sure she was becoming part of the tree itself. In all the years he'd known her, he never knew she was a hamadryad. But then she was always full of surprises, he thought, as his legs pounded the ground desperately.

'At least she's safe. At least she's safe,' he reposted in his head as his feet struggled to cope with a flower bed and then some wet grass. Winded, Sam finally fell head first at the foot of a tree. He was too exhausted to climb up it but struggled to stand up, his back pressed against the trunk.

The wolf was almost upon him now. It stopped a few yards away, fangs bared, creeping forward paw by paw. The animal pressed closer, huge clouds of steam issuing from its mouth and nostrils. 'This time they've won!' thought Sam and prepared for the pain that was about to begin.

As his heart hammered in his chest, he realised that the animal had stopped. It simply stood there, its lupine lips moving strangely as if it was trying to speak. After a few moments Sam could hear faint whispering and peered more closely at the animal's mouth. Eventually he gained enough courage to lean closer to the wolf.

" ... that no such undertaking has been received and that, consequently, this country is at war with Germany."

Sam couldn't believe what he was hearing. Then, even though the sky was clear with not an aircraft in sight, he knew what it must mean. 'Oh, shit!" he gasped and looked around desperately for shelter of some sort. The rising shriek of air-raid sirens reached his ears as two trees across the park were torn apart in a violent burst of flame.

He was getting ready to run, heading towards the bridge across the brook that ran along the edge of the park, when he realised that the enormous wolf was blocking his way. His mind raced, trying to think of a way to get past the enormous brute, as a series of explosions crept nearer to him second by second.

He could no longer hear the wolf's heavy panting and turned to look at the creature. It was no longer moving; its fur had become stiff and grey, its eyes now dull and lifeless. Sam stretched out his hand and touched the animal's huge muzzle. It was stone.

The only feeling he had for his former persecutor was now gratitude as he saw there was just enough room under the beast's shaggy belly for him. He scrambled between the giant stone paws just as another series of bomb bursts tore up the gravel path and scattered clods of earth around him. He closed his eyes in pain as the roar hammered into his ears, the vibration set to shake his head loose and send it rolling away across the park. He clutched one of the wolf's front legs, panting hard.

After some minutes, Sam opened his eyes and rubbed away the tears that were streaming down his cheeks. His head ached and everything sounded as if it was under water. He shook his head and dug his fingers in his ears. He opened his mouth to yawn. But his hearing refused to return to normal.

He walked across the park to the tree where he'd last seen Helen. The ground had been churned up by a huge explosion. The tree was no longer there.

He searched around on the ground for some splinters. 'I've lost her again,' he thought and then struggled to remind himself that she'd never really been there. He still couldn't stop himself from collecting some tiny fragments of wood and putting them in his pocket.

His ears still ringing, Sam drifted across the bridge and out of the park, finding himself in a slightly less run-down section of this unreal town. Day and night seemed to come and go with depressing regularity, he thought, as darkness closed in once more.

In the sky there was something that was either a quarter moon, a curved blade or a silver-skinned fish twisting back on itself. He began to walk down a likely-looking street. But when he caught a glimpse of a big top beyond the far end of the street, and a spangled girl riding an elephant, he turned on his heels.

At the end of the street, he passed a bus shelter. In it stood a woman in dark glasses. Next to her was a surgeon complete with his leather medical bag; he had a hump on his back. Then there was a man carrying a huge pair of scissors, which Sam assumed was an advertising gimmick.

All three were asleep standing up. Sam stood and shouted 'Hello' several times before losing patience and carrying on his way. At least I can hear myself now, he thought, grateful that his hearing was returning.

He became drowsy and felt as though he was sleeping. He didn't wonder whether it was possible to sleep inside a dream, he merely dozed and drifted. When he next looked up he was in a part of town he didn't recognise. Then he reminded himself that he was in a town he'd never visited before and would never be able to visit again. The sun had come up remarkably quickly and now it was early morning.

The street was lined on both sides with glass-fronted buildings, all reflecting each other and nothing else. When Sam walked up to the front of one, his reflection barely registered; he was merely a whisper of a ghost in the glass.

He looked up, but there was nothing to see except bright glass reflecting bright glass - which seemed to grow brighter with each passing moment - and a vaguely blue sky in the narrow gap left between the tops of the buildings.

Then Sam registered some movement in this wilderness of shining shards. High up on one of the buildings, he was sure he saw something clinging to the vertical face of the glass. But if there was, he thought, then it must be glass, too, because he couldn't make out any colour. Just a vague insect-like form, clinging there, unmoving.

Until suddenly it jumped at enormous speed, from a standstill, and went through one of the buildings. Sam drew in his breath, making a cartoon gasping sound, and rushed to the next road junction to see where the thing had gone.

He peered up for several seconds before spotting it. From this angle he could see more clearly, even though he actually saw through it. There was a large-ish head at the end of a slender body and those distinctive long legs told him at once what the thing must be. It was an enormous glasshopper. And that gave Sam an idea.

Pulling back his shirt sleeve, he was relieved to see that his watch was still in one piece. Using his other cuff he cleaned the grime off the glass covering the watch face. Lifting his arm, he carefully angled it so the small disc caught the light of the sun. He peered up at the side of the building where the glasshopper sat, his eyes aching with the brightness. It was hard for him to see it at first but eventually he picked up the moving circle of light.

Moving his arm back-and-forth only a fraction of an inch, he aimed it at the place where the thing's eyes must be. The insect twitched a rear leg and inclined its head towards Sam. It seemed to be getting agitated.

Within seconds Sam was bombarded with sunlight as the creature leapt towards him and landed a few feet away. It stood about seven feet tall, moving its head from side to side, trying to decide what it was looking at. Sam held out his hand to pat the side of the transparent creature's head. He knew this worked with horses but he'd had no experience with giant insects.

The glasshopper reacted favourably. It twitched its huge mandibles only when it was pointing away from Sam, which he took as a good sign. After a few minutes, Sam carefully slipped his trouser belt out of its loops. Making sure to continue his patting motion, he moved around the side of the insect.

It would be tricky but there was enough room to sit between the giant legs. If he could climb on top of it, he could ride the glasshopper.

The insect seemed to be asleep as Sam carefully placed one foot on a section of its right leg. The textured sole of his shoe gripped better than he'd hoped for and soon he was lying on the creature's back. It didn't move as he slipped his belt around what passed for its neck with some difficulty. His arms were at full stretch and still the belt only just reached around the beast.

The still insect merely sat there. How do I get it to move, wondered Sam. 'Home, James,' he muttered. The insect twitched its back legs, pitching itself and its passenger forward. Sam screwed his eyes shut and concentrated on his house, his bed, his sedentary life.

Sam's stomach left his body as the huge thing leapt into the air. The glasshopper clung to the side of a building, clacking its mandibles. Sam opened his eyes and was met with a dizzying vista. He didn't know how but he was defying gravity, too.

The beast flexed its legs again and then they were airborne once more. Sam opened one eye and saw that they were headed towards a very solid-looking wall of glass that ran across the street, blocking their way.

Sam covered his face with his arm and ducked his head as low as he could. As the giant insect hit the wall with a tremendous shuddering smash, a rain of dreamglass and mindshards fell over them both. They landed with an alarming jerking motion and Sam immediately slid off the creature's back, landing uncomfortably on one knee.

He found himself on a roundabout. It was mainly grass with some shrubs and trees that had been added by an eager landscape gardener. The shattered glass wall ran through the centre of it. Cars roared around him and the air was thick with exhaust fumes. Over to one side was a large supermarket, which he recognised as being a few miles from his house. Sam smiled.

The huge insect looked down at Sam, then flexed its tremendous rear legs and leapt into the air. Sam tried to follow it with his eyes but it was gone in a sudden sharp glint of sunlight, lost for good in the desert of summer blue overhead. He imagined the insect had hopped too close to the sun and melted away.

From behind the remnants of the fading wall, he heard a voice. Turning to face his erstwhile tormentor, Sam spat on the ground and brushed a few tiny shards of glass from his hair. As they touched his palm, they became hazy wisps of nothing, soon gone.

"Well done, Sam. Well done. See you again next year." Sparing Sam the obvious demonic cackle, the old man simply turned his back and walked away. After several steps, Sam could see the cars through him, then he too was gone.

The wall faded completely, taking with it any suggestion that this was anything other than a boring roundabout on the edge of town.

Sam was left with a tremendous headache and a sense that today had never begun but would also never end. I need a couple of paracetamol, he thought.

Then, remembering something that he'd somehow never forgotten, he fished into his pocket and came out with a handful of dust and emptiness. But at least he was awake and that was a good thing. He hoped.

These stories were first published in the Manchester-based literary magazine *Sein und Werden*. Plus 'The Circus Of Automatic Dreams', commissioned especially for this book.

Made in the USA
Middletown, DE
11 March 2017